Little Little

OTHER BOOKS BY M. E. KERR

Gentlehands
I'll Love You When You're More Like Me
Love Is a Missing Person
Is That You, Miss Blue?
The Son of Someone Famous
If I Love You, Am I Trapped Forever?
Dinky Hocker Shoots Smack!

M.E. KERR
Little Little

Harper & Row, Publishers

NEW YORK

Cambridge London
Hagerstown Mexico City
Philadelphia São Paulo
San Francisco Sydney

1817

Little Little
Copyright © 1981 by M. E. Kerr
All rights reserved. No part of this book may be
used or reproduced in any manner whatsoever without
written permission except in the case of brief
quotations embodied in critical articles and reviews.
Printed in the United States of America.
For information address Harper & Row, Publishers, Inc.,
10 East 53rd Street, New York, N.Y. 10022.
Published simultaneously in Canada by
Fitzhenry & Whiteside Limited, Toronto.
First Edition

Library of Congress Cataloging in Publication Data
Kerr, M E
    Little Little.
    SUMMARY: The shenanigans of two dwarfs as
they compete for the heart of Little Little, a
dwarf heiress who's tired of being treated like
a pretty doll.
    [1. Dwarfs—Fiction] I. Title.
PZ7.K46825Li 1981   [Fic]   80-8454
ISBN 0-06-023184-X
ISBN 0-06-023185-8 (lib. bdg.)

For Mildred Greenwald
—Millie—
Always new
&
For Alison and Thor—
Old friends are Gold

Little Little

Sydney Cinnamon

"Sydney," Mr. Palmer said, "you are on your way to becoming the most famous dwarf in this country, no small thanks to me. And now I have a favor to ask you."

Those words, spoken on an ordinary August day, in the offices of Palmer Pest Control, were the beginning of my new life.

So far, age seventeen, I had had two other beginnings.

One was my birth and abandonment to The Twin Oaks Orphans' Home in Wilton, New York.

One was my first appearance as The Roach, mascot for the Wilton Bombers, at halftime during the first game of the year. I was fifteen, and though I didn't know it at the time, it was to be the last year I'd attend Wilton High School.

"Sydney Cinnamon," Mr. Palmer said that morning in his office, "with everything against you, you made yourself into something. You created a self for yourself. You are

The Roach, an entity of your own invention, and I admire you for it. I have something along the same order in mind for myself."

"What are you planning to become?" I asked him.

"I'm not planning to become anything. I'm planning on Palmer Pest Control becoming something. I want to go national, Sydney! I want to be big!" Mr. Palmer looked like an enormous bird, like the kind of huge, skinny, long-beaked bird that swooped down from the sky, poked around in the dirt, and carried away the very creatures Mr. Palmer exterminated for a living.

"Sydney," he said, rubbing his palms together ecstatically, "I'm negotiating with a Japanese named Hiroyuki for a merger with Twinkle Traps, over in La Belle, New York. Together, Twinkle and Palmer could control the market. I need your help, Sydney."

He knew he could ask me to do anything. Because of him, I had changed from an orphaned dwarf who picked up odd jobs jumping out of birthday cakes, or working summers at resorts like Leprechaun Village, to a TV personality who earned enough money to finally order clothes made that fit, and furniture my own size.

The commercials I made for P.P.C., as The Roach, were famous in upstate New York. If Mr. Palmer had exaggerated slightly in saying I was on my way to becoming the most famous dwarf in the country, it still did not take away from the fact I had my own little fame wherever I went.

And fame is fame. The big fish in the little pond doesn't

bother its head about larger bodies of water. Thanks to Albert Palmer, I'd gone from entertaining as The Roach at halftime in high school football fields to making commercials and appearing at shopping centers, and starring at openings of everything from bowling alleys to cut-rate liquor stores.

I even had my own theme song, which was "La Cucaracha," and my own groupies, kids who congregated wherever I appeared, and waved pieces of paper at me that they wanted me to autograph.

"I'll do anything you say," I told Mr. Palmer, and he rubbed his bald head and grinned at me, then came around and sat on the front of his desk, facing me.

"The last week in September," he said, "the Wilton Bombers are playing the La Belle Boots, at La Belle. Sydney, I'd like you to make an appearance at halftime. It's a way to tell our home team you haven't forgotten your beginnings, and we're still in there rooting for them. And it's a way to show you off in La Belle."

"That's easy," I said.

"And the second part isn't going to be hard, either. There's a surprise in it for you, Sydney, one I think you'll like. She's your size, Sydney."

"Who?"

"They call her Little Little La Belle. She's one of the little people, like you, and she's the daughter of Larry La Belle. Of course, his family is very prominent in that town, town's named for them. She's having her eighteenth birthday party that weekend, and Mr. Hiroyuki would like you to make a little surprise guest appearance at the party. His boy's a friend of the family, and that'd be his gift to this little girl.''

''It's all right with me,'' I said.

''You'll be a surprise for the little lady, and it'll help me get Hiroyuki in a good mood when we talk merger.''

I said I would and then I began wangling for the very best accommodations while I was in La Belle.

I'd learned to do that from a fellow named Knox Lionel. We'd roomed together in the employees' dormitory at Leprechaun Village, the summer we both worked there. Knox was seventeen that summer and I was fourteen. He was a combination philosopher and con man, who loved to watch the TV preachers and imitate them. He entertained us in the dorm posing as a preacher called Opportunity Knox, a mixture of all the television preachers he'd studied. He could cry like Jimmy Swaggart. He could fret like Rex Humbard. He could beam like Robert Schuller and shake a pointed finger like Billy Graham. He stood on a box to deliver sermons on sin that had us holding our sides laughing.

But he wasn't kidding when he preached about sticking up for ourselves.

''When you go on a job,'' Knox always said, ''make sure your little ass goes first class! You never know how a job's going to turn out for you. Some jobs you'll fend off drunks or ladies who want to hold you on their laps or dogs who want to knock you over and lick your face. Make sure ahead

4

of time you've got first-class accommodations. If you don't stick up for yourself, you'll go from jobs like that back to some fleabag with the head down the hall."

Everything a dwarf needed to figure out, Knox had figured out. Even though he didn't have a hump like some of us, and was this miniature marvel of a good-looking guy, he never called himself a midget or a little person.

He'd stand on his box and shout, "The word is 'dwarf'!"

He'd lecture us that blacks didn't get anywhere calling themselves "colored" or "Negro": that all of us were duty bound to call ourselves the worst thing anyone could call us: *dwarf*—"And make it beautiful!" he'd roar.

He was the only dwarf I'd ever met whose mother and father had been dwarfs, too, though I'd heard of a few such cases. There was a dwarf who'd played in a major league baseball game who'd had dwarf parents. He was Edward Gaedel and he'd played one game for the St. Louis Browns in 1951, as a stunt. But the vast majority of us are flukes in our families.

Knox had appeared in an act with his folks in a series of second-rate carnivals, where they were billed as The Inch Family. He was also the only dwarf in Leprechaun Village who'd been earning his living since he could walk, in one form or another of sleazy show business, until both his parents died. He liked to dress all in white, and said it was because of all the years he could never wear white, when he was working carnies in dusty lots, or on the road for weeks with no place to get his clothes cleaned.

5

Some of them in the dorm didn't like him; some were fascinated by him; all agreed he had the smarts, and we called him "Opportunity."

There was a time in Skaneateles, New York, where I'd been sent away from a job on a cold February night because the hostess of the Valentine party hadn't been told I had a hump. She said there was no way I could play Cupid, since I was supposed to appear practically naked. Anyway, she said, Cupid wasn't a hunchback. Instead of the hundred dollars I'd been promised, in addition to a hotel room and meals, she gave me a twenty, and said to please leave before the guests arrived.

Later on in my large, comfortable room at The Skaneateles Inn, feasting on filet mignon and watching the snow fall on Skaneateles Lake, I gave silent thanks to Opportunity Knox.

I also learned, from then on, always to mention the hump, though later, as The Roach, that never mattered. I had my plastic shell covering me as I performed.

Mr. Palmer said, "Sydney, you'll *have* a room with a view, color TV, a separate bath—nothing but the best! You'll be put up at the Stardust Inn. I'm staying there myself!"

Although I'd never been in La Belle, New York, I knew about the Inn. As a youngster, I'd gone with others from Twin Oaks for an outing at an amusement park on the outskirts of La Belle: Stardust Park.

"Okay," I said. "I'm glad to do it."

6

"Sydney," he said, getting off his desk, "La Belle has a fine library, too."

The few times we'd traveled anywhere together, I often had Mr. Palmer leave me at the local library while he took care of business.

I was comfortable in libraries, and reading was my passion.

Once, on a job, when I jumped out of a cold cherry pie at a George Washington's Birthday bachelor party, the guest of honor and I got talking.

He told me he was a psychologist, and he wanted to question me about my life-style. He was drunk—they always are at bachelor parties—and when he found out how much I read, he leaned into me and suggested, "You're overcompenshating, Shydney."

"For what?"

"For being sho short," he said. "You want to know sho much sho people forget your shize." Before he fell face down into his plate he added, "You esh-esh-cape that way, too."

After I became The Roach, I read even more, and then I think I was overcompensating, not for being a dwarf, but for being a high school dropout.

That was something I didn't thank Opportunity Knox for; it was his example I'd followed. He used to tell us all we needed was to *say* that we'd graduated from high school. "You can fake it!" he'd say. "You can fake anything!"

Once he told me, "We can't walk to where we've got to

get, Sydney, because our dear little legs won't get us there as fast as the competition's. So we've got to jump!"

In his room at the dorm in Leprechaun Village he had one of those signs that said T H I N K. T H I N K had been crossed out, and H U S T L E had been written over it. Then H U S T L E had been crossed out, and S C H E M E! had been written over that.

Mr. Palmer shook my hand. "Sydney, then it's settled? You'll make your appearance at halftime, do the guest shot for the little La Belle girl's party, and I want you to have dinner with Mr. Hiroyuki and me one night. The rest of the time you're on your own. . . . Do you still read and watch TV at the same time?"

"Yes," I said. "That way I don't miss anything."

"From my way of looking at it, you miss two very important things," said Mr. Palmer. "You miss the point of what you're reading and the point of what you're watching."

He laughed and slapped my back, and we started toward the door together.

I remembered something else from my days at Leprechaun Village: a dwarf with bad legs, like mine, whom we called Artoo-Detoo, because he walked like the robot in the old film *Star Wars*.

"Imagine thinking back to a time when you were another size!" Artoo-Detoo would exclaim. "Imagine growing out of your clothes—waking up one morning and your wrists have jumped past your shirt sleeves!"

I watched myself in the wall of mirrors at the end of Mr.

8

Palmer's office. I thought of the time I had visited Stardust Park. I was eleven then. Yet very little about my physical appearance had changed in those six years.

Three foot four and a half, still . . . the same hump, not bigger, not smaller. Legs too short for my body. My face could pass for normal. Light blue eyes, fair teeth except for one that hung like a fang longer than the others, bucking out from the row, sandy-colored hair, good skin . . . but the rest of me was like God'd gone mad when He started making me from the neck down.

"So long, Sydney," Mr. Palmer said in the doorway. "See you in September. In La Belle."

Little Little La Belle

YOU ARE INVITED TO A PARTY

Get out your drum and fife and fiddle,
We're giving a party for Little Little,
On a September weekend here in La Belle,
Reserve a room at The Lakeside Motel,
There'll be lots to do on Sat. and Sun.
A banquet, a movie, and other fun.
It's a TADpole party for our little queen,
It's a birthday party, she'll be eighteen!
                    —*Ava Hancock La Belle*

Once when my sister, Cowboy, was little, she asked me why I wasn't "throwed away" when I was born.

"I wasn't throwed away," I told her, "because no one knew then that I was different."

"Wasn't you littler than anybody?"

"No, I wasn't."

"You was funny-looking, though, wasn't you?"

"I never looked better," I said.

That is a fact. I was a normal baby, even a big one—nine pounds and two ounces at birth. I had my mother's golden hair and my father's light green eyes.

I don't think my sister ever stops asking herself that question, though we are thick as thieves now and united against a world that is barking mad.

Still, it has been a blight on Cowboy's life that the town dwarf is her older sister.

My mother has this thing about certain words and one of them is "pee."

She says don't say pee. I say I hate the word "urinate," it's so official-sounding for something you do with your pants down. Why do you have to use either word? she asks me. Say I have to go to the bathroom if you have to say anything, or say you'd like to wash up. My father says just say excuse me. Or just say I'll be right back.

You *could* say something fun, my father says, like I have to spend a penny, or see a man about a dog. My mother brightens at this prospect and says when *I* was in high school I said I have to use the Kitty Litter or I have to tinkle. Now they start together enthusiastically, their eyes shining with the pleasure of finding a way to avoid saying I have to

pee or I have to urinate. . . . *Où est le WC?* I have to use
the head. I'm going to the john. I've got to see Mrs. Jones.
I have to powder my nose. I have to pay a visit to the ladies'.
I have an errand. I'm going to the little girls'. I have to make
wee-wee. I have to go to the loo. On and on.

Another word my mother cannot stand is "dwarf."

"Don't say 'dwarf,' " my mother says. "Call yourself a
little person or a midget or a diminutive. Anything but
'dwarf.' "

That's why I prefer to call myself a dwarf.

"You picture someone with a hump when you hear the
word 'dwarf,' " my mother whines at me.

I tell her, "One person's picture is another person's child.
There are probably people who picture cone-headed
gnomes when they hear the words 'little person' or 'midget'
or 'diminutive.' "

"No, no, no, a little person or a midget or a diminutive
is just a very small person, like you, Little Little, perfectly
formed and perfectly beautiful."

"If I'm so perfect, what does it matter what I call myself?"

"Well, Little Little, your mouth isn't perfect."

"What's wrong with my mouth?"

"It's always open, seems to me, and there's always something sassy coming out of it."

My mother has been trying for nearly eighteen years to
have a sense of humor about it. She treats Life as though it
were some great force even larger than God. God gets the
credit for everything good that happens, but anything bad

or bewildering that happens causes her to exclaim, "Well what is Life going to do to us next!"

Giving birth to someone like me is a little like falling off a horse. The very best thing you can do is get right back on one as quickly as possible, so you lose your fear of horses. Which explains why my sister was hustled into being very soon after my mother's reeling head was just beginning to assimilate the knowledge I'd never stand taller on two feet than the family dog did on four.

At five months I weighed fifteen pounds and two ounces and was two feet one inch tall. At the end of a year my weight and height were exactly the same.

Cowboy was born when I was two, and though I grew a little more, at ten I stopped growing. Cowboy was eight and towering over me. I stood, and still stand, three feet three inches tall.

My real name is Belle La Belle, but I have always been called Little Little by everyone, even teachers.

Cowboy's real name is Emily, and only teachers ever call her that.

Cowboy was supposed to have been the long-awaited boy, Larry La Belle, Jr.

All the things my father planned to do with the long-awaited boy were done instead with Cowboy.

She has gone through many stages.

The one in which she earned her nickname went on from

the time she was four until she was eleven. She rode horseback before her feet were long enough to reach the stirrups, and rode her bicycle as though it were a stallion, jumping off it after she flew into our front yard, letting it clatter ahead and crash into the garage wall, while she walked coolly away from it as though it were standing patiently saddled awaiting her return. Inside our house, I was always the Indian, being pursued by her and lassoed, our mother screaming after her not to wear her hat in the house, not to pull the rope too tight around my neck, "REMOVE THOSE SPURS YOU'LL SCRATCH THE FURNITURE!"

Long after she was out of chaps and boots, she had a thing for horses (and still does, though it does her no good, my father won't buy her one). She went on for a while to her sports stage. Anything that bounced or could be thrown and caught was all she cared about. She spent long hours in the den with my father in the blue light of the boob tube cheering on men with first names like Bucky and Buzz, her dinner served on a tray the same as my father's.

The death and suicide stage came in her early teens and was a disguised way of protesting having to have anything to do with me outside our home. She took to her bed rather than have to wait for me in front of school, or sit with me in the cafeteria, or say I was her sister.

Now it is hard to tell which one of us is most strange, me or Cowboy, though a dwarf will always look stranger anywhere.

Cowboy doesn't wear her ten-gallon hat and chaps to school anymore, but in other ways she lives up to her name. She is tall enough to be sought out by the La Belle High girls' basketball team (the only ones at school who seek her out) and walks as though she just got off the horse she wishes she owned. She spits sometimes, swears she doesn't, but she stops and hawks into the gutters—I've seen her do it. And she smokes Camel cigarettes with no hands. A Camel dangles from her mouth at all times away from home and school, and she lopes around like some tall farm boy coming in from the wheat fields. Her hair is all tight curls, to her shoulders, and tangled, never combed. She claims a comb won't go through it. Whatever she says comes out of the corner of her mouth. Her shy smiles are always tipped and she rarely shows teeth when smiling. I imagine that she smells of hay and manure, not a bad smell but a musky one my mother says is all in my head: "No one else smells Cowboy, Little Little."

Cowboy likes to laugh with her hands in her pockets and her head thrown back, and when she's not relaxed she cracks her knuckles.

"When is Life going to straighten you around!" my mother cries at her, and hugs her, says, "Oh, Cowboy, you are *something*, aren't you?"

Our little town in the Finger Lakes, upstate New York, has been partially saved from economic disaster by the arrival of the Twinkle Traps plant, which is Japanese-owned. And Cowboy has been saved from being ostracized by nearly everyone except the girls' basketball team, by glomming onto Mock Hiroyuki, a Japanese boy her same age, fifteen, new to our town and the country's customs.

Cowboy is now in her Japanese stage.

She enters our house calling out *"Kon-nici-wa,"* and leaves with *"Sayonara!"*

If we ever need Cowboy for anything, we know she is at the Hiroyukis'.

Sydney Cinnamon 3

I was always a sentimental fellow. My eyes teared at the memories of old times and leaked at the sounds of old songs recalling past days with friends I never saw anymore. I had favorite places, too, and one of them was Stardust Park.

Immediately after I checked into The Stardust Inn that hot Friday afternoon in September, I walked down to the park, even though I knew it was closed because it was off season.

Stardust Park was only thirty miles from The Twin Oaks Orphans' Home.

When I was at Twin Oaks, I lived in Miss Lake's cottage, where most of the handicapped lived. There were ramps for wheelchairs there instead of stairs, and sinks and closets and drinking fountains, et cetera, were lower to accommodate us.

All the kids who lived in Miss Lake's called it Mistakes.

There was every kind of kid to be expected there, but I was the only dwarf.

Stardust Park in the summer was a miniature Disneyland, filled with all the things you'd find in one of those places, from a 62-MPH roller coaster to a ten-foot walking chicken.

I was taken there one time with some others from Mistakes, just as the sun was rising in the early morning sky.

We always went to public places before the public was allowed in.

Some of the employees who ran the rides and sold the souvenirs were sitting around having their morning coffee.

Even though they were supposed to be prepared for the visit from Twin Oaks, they didn't look it. Their heads whirled around as we filed past them, and I said under my breath, "MyGoddoyouseewhatIsee?"

I always said what everyone watching us was thinking when we came into view. OhmyGoddoyouseewhatIsee?

There was me, and there was Wheels Potter, who had no legs and got about on a board with roller-skate wheels attached to it. There was Bighead Langhorn, whose head was the size of an enormous pumpkin set on a skinny body just a little taller than mine. There was Wires Kaplan, with his hearing aid and his thick glasses and his bum leg. There was Cloud, the one-armed albino, in his dark glasses with his massive head of curly white hair the texture of steel wool. There was Pill Suchanek, whose mother had taken some drug before Pill was born that threw her whole body out of whack and left her with flippers for arms. There were a few in wheelchairs and one on crutches, all led by a teacher we had nicknamed Robot, because his first name was Robert and his only facial expression was a smile, his only mood cheerful.

I paid very little attention to The Underground City or the ten-foot chicken, the 62-MPH roller coaster, The Space Shuttle, The Early American Village, or Winter Wonderland.

I had gone on that expedition expressly to see Gnomeland.

Age eleven, I had never seen another dwarf, except on television or in drawings and photographs.

When I entered Gnomeland, I could not believe my eyes. It didn't matter to me that they were all dressed in cute little costumes with bells attached to stocking caps and felt shoes on their feet, that the men wore fake white beards and some of the men and women wore cone-shaped red hats.

I laughed aloud at the buttons some wore proclaiming THERE'S NO PLACE LIKE GNOME.

I saw some with humps and some without, some wizened and ugly and some not, some old, some young—they all looked good to me.

I imagined (or I didn't) that they were all smiling at me especially, as though we all shared a fantastic secret.

Still, shyly, I stayed by Robot, who must have read my bashfulness as some sort of reluctance.

"Are you bothered by this, Sydney?"

"Bothered?"

"By this . . . commercialization?"

"I'm not bothered," I told him, not really sure what he

was talking about. I added, "Anything but," longing to speak to one of them, to get my nerve up to say something.

But all I managed was a futile tug at the arm of Robot's coat when he said all right, next was the boat ride through The Underground City.

"Come on, Sydney!" Robot called as I fell behind. "Get ready to row row row your boat!"

A hunchback dwarf with a fat cigar in his mouth stood at a microphone singing, "You're gnomebody 'til somebody loves you. . . ."

I believed that I had died and gone to heaven.

When I got back to Twin Oaks, I wrote to Gnomeland, asking how old you had to be to get a job there, and enclosed a stamped self-addressed envelope to be sure of an answer.

I remember you but stay in school, a Mr. T. Kamitses wrote back. *Get an etucation. Anyways, this is the last year Gnomeland will be at Stardust Park, for our contrack was not renewed. Good luck!*

I kept the letter. Even with its bad news and bad spelling it was the only communication I'd ever had with another like me.

Six years later, walking through Stardust Park, I thought about that day.

That day was the beginning of when I knew I'd make it.

Of course I knew she was Little Little La Belle the instant I saw her by the shuttered cotton candy stand.

I was walking along, looking for some sign of the trailer camp mentioned in this note awaiting me when I'd checked in at The Stardust Inn:

Hey, Roach, remember your old buddy Digger Starr? Me and Laura Gwen got married and now have twin daughters. I'm playing my last year for The Bombers. We got a trailer parked in the trailer camp near the park if you can make dinner Fri. night about 7. Our rig is the silver one with the babies yelling inside (ha! ha!) so show up for a special dinner in honor of the sellebrity. (You.) It will be swell to see you so show up from your old buddy, D.S.

If I had to go anywhere at night, I liked to figure out my route ahead of time. I looked for well-lighted bus stops and streets with stores along the route, figuring out any moves I might be forced to make by gangs of kids, or a dog, or a mugger.

If the trailer park was close to the Inn, I planned to take a taxi, and this was what I was working on when I saw her.

I had a chance to look at her before she spotted me. Aside from Dora, who appeared on national television as The Dancing Lettuce Leaf in the Melody Mayonnaise commercials, she was the most beautiful dwarf I'd ever seen.

I'd only seen Dora on the tube, watching sometimes for hours to catch a glimpse of her, so Little Little La Belle was the most beautiful dwarf I'd ever seen in person.

If I had conjured up an ideal female out of my imagination, I couldn't have surpassed what I saw standing by COTTON CANDY in the late afternoon sunlight. She had long blond hair that shined and spilled down past her oulders, and unlike the girls at Leprechaun Village she wore a dress instead of pants. She had long legs for someone so tiny, and she was thin and still tanned from summer.

The great disadvantage of being The Roach was that, without my shell, few people knew that was who I was. Some of my groupies who waited for me regularly when I made appearances had come to know me without it, but mostly I was an anonymous dwarf.

I think I am by nature a performer, and away from the hot lights of local TV stations, or the crowds at some place like The Golden Dragon (in long lines to receive one free fortune cookie in honor of its opening), I am not pushy. I see my hump reflected in watery patterns of store windows and pull my sweater down where it rides up in back, and cover my buck fang with my hand. I have my downs.

They pass. I am normally noisy, dancing to my radio and tapes in my room over Palmer Pest Control, cracking jokes and amiable around people, and in my daydreams stepping before the footlights like Michael Dunn, who played the dwarf in the movie *Ship of Fools.* Sometimes I see myself beating a tiny tin drum like Oskar in Günter Grass's book . . . and sometimes in my act I sing under my shell, imagining myself singing windowpanes to pieces as Oskar did. I am a closet tenor who dreams of stepping out of his closet, and out from under the shell, to thrill the crowds with "Danny Boy."

When Little Little La Belle finally did look in my direction, she looked hard and directly at me, and that was when I might have nodded, waved, smiled. I froze instead. I stayed so still she might have mistaken me for one of those wooden trolls people buy at garden centers and stick on their lawns. Except I was standing in the middle of a cement sidewalk outside of the penny arcade.

I could feel my face get red, and I looked away, demonstrating at least that my head moved.

By the time I glanced up at her again, she had started walking in the opposite direction.

I followed, not at a fast pace, but I went in the same direction she was going.

I knew she'd take a second look. We dwarfs come upon each other about as often as fish nest in trees, unless we're all working together someplace. I planned a friendly wave that I couldn't seem to bring my arms to execute, so when she sneaked a glance over her shoulder through her long golden hair, I merely trudged along in line with her, my arms paralyzed.

She walked faster. I didn't want to charge after her in hot pursuit like some dwarf rapist on the loose. I finally stood near the 62-MPH roller coaster, as stopped in my tracks as it was.

When I was at Leprechaun Village, after a day's work (we emptied ashtrays, brought pillows down poolside, paged people wanted on the telephone, ran errands, and got drinks from the bar) every night I would watch Opportunity Knox get dressed for a date. He was popular not only with other dwarfs but with normal-sized females as well. One night he slipped off for a very secret rendezvous with a guest, the wife of an Italian count, who gave him a gold signet ring inscribed *Amoretta.* That same night I had trudged along to a local movie with a group of other employees, envying his luck.

"It isn't luck, Sydney!" he'd insist. "Fate loves the fearless! Happiness hates the timid! Are you going to miss the plum because you're afraid to shake the tree? Are you always going to be the anvil, and never the hammer?"

I stood there remembering that, doing hypnosis on Little Little La Belle's back as she walked along: *You will look my way again!*

It took her around twenty seconds to register my message, to turn and take another look, and I got ready for my one little puff of a gesture. There was no small effort involved, either, with my hump, which was the reason I'd perfected the stunt years ago, so that my feet went off the ground like flying.

She gave a look and I gave back: a cartwheel.

Back on my feet, I saw she was still watching me, and with one arm across my stomach, and one behind me an inch from my hump, I bowed low.

Little Little La Belle 4

When I was growing up, it was my Grandfather La Belle who gave me names like Richard Gibson, famous painter and most famous miniaturist in all the world . . . Toulouse-Lautrec, whose paintings were priceless and in every major museum . . . Attila the Hun, who led an army of half a million across Europe . . . Croesus, king of Lydia in Asia Minor, from whom we get the expression "rich as Croesus" . . . and Richebourg, a spy in the French Revolution. On and on.

"All little people!" he would bellow. "All famous!"

When I asked him where the female dwarfs were, he said they were buried in history along with other notable ladies. He said they were there all right, he just didn't happen to know about them.

He'd done a lot of research in the La Belle library and seemed always to have new names for me of other important dwarfs, with one omission.

"Why don't you ever tell me about Tom Thumb?" I asked him.

"Oh, Tom Thumb," he answered disdainfully.

"I've been reading a lot about him. He was very successful. He was a general and—"

"He was a general of nothing! He was given the title General by a fellow who had a circus. P. T. Barnum! He wasn't a real general."

"But he was the most famous dwarf in the world, wasn't he?"

"He was paraded around."

"He met Queen Victoria and the Duke of Wellington and the Prince of Wales. He even met President Lincoln."

"He might have done all that without being a dwarf."

"How?"

"How?" my grandfather said. "By using what he had up here"—tapping his forehead with his finger—"instead of letting someone exploit him!"

"What does 'exploit' mean, Grandfather?"

"It means to utilize for profit. This Barnum fellow made a lot of money satisfying the public's curiosity about what someone different looks like. He turned Tom Thumb into a sideshow!"

"Didn't he pay him?"

"Oh, he paid him. But that's no way to live your life, Little Little, and he's no example to follow!"

Long after I needed to be burped, my grandfather would

26

hold me in his arm tightly, jiggling me up and down the way you do a baby, and reciting into my ear:

> *If you can't be a pine on top of the hill,*
> *Be a scrub in the valley—but be*
> *The best little scrub by the side of the rill;*
> *Be a bush if you can't be a tree.*

They were soothing words to hear being danced around my room, until I grew old enough to think them over and decide that the idea of being a bush wasn't all that appealing, and for me, anyway, not the answer, even if I was best bush.

Except for Calpurnia Dove, I am the best writer in Miss Grossman's English class.

Miss Grossman usually chooses to read aloud either something I have written or something Calpurnia has written. We are always neck and neck in the race.

When something Calpurnia wrote is read, I decide Miss Grossman is only being nice to her because Calpurnia is black, and mine is really better. Something tells me that when what I wrote is read, Calpurnia Dove decides Miss Grossman is only being nice to me because I'm a dwarf, and hers is really better.

There are not many black families in La Belle, or in Cayuta County. We are even uncertain about calling them "blacks" and still slip back at times to "Negro," "colored," worse.

Our downtown restaurants have more blacks waiting on tables than sitting at tables to be waited on, and more blacks than that in the kitchen with their hands in the dishwater.

What black teenagers there are in La Belle go mostly to Commercial High, to learn trades or business skills. Of the few that go to La Belle High, one is always elected to some office, unanimously. But that high honor rarely gets one of them a seat saved at noon in the cafeteria among the whites, or even a particularly warm hello.

Calpurnia Dove is the treasurer of our senior class, the only senior in the whole school who's black.

That Friday afternoon of my big birthday weekend, the assignment for Miss Grossman's class had been to write a short story.

I'd written one called "The Wistful Wheel," about a wheel who longed to travel alone, but always had to be attached to something to move.

When I read it to Cowboy, she said, "This isn't about a wheel. It's about you, Little Little. You always hated traveling with the family."

I hadn't intended it to be about me, but maybe Cowboy was right. Maybe Miss Grossman was right, too, about what a fantasy was. She said when you wrote a fantasy you were like a spider spinning a web from your own insides.

Whenever our family went anywhere, we were always stared at because of me. There were always what Cowboy and I called "peepers" in the hotel dining room, or the motel lobbies. Wherever we went, we'd see them looking over the tops of their newspapers or menus, stealing glances when they thought we weren't watching, sometimes just plain staring at us as though we'd just piled out of a flying saucer direct from Mars.

"Jeepers creepers, look at all the peepers," Cowboy would remark.

She'd try her best to laugh it off, but she'd get red and start cracking her knuckles, and I'd wish I'd just eaten in my room, or not gone on the trip at all.

My mother'd purr, "You have to expect to be admired when you're such an extraordinary little beauty, darling."

But she'd knock back a double martini to get past it, and my father's face would be fixed in a scowl, his angry eyes trying to meet with the peepers' eyes to stare them down.

Except when we were all tooling along together in the car, I never really saw the sights when we went places. I saw the sightseers see me.

That afternoon in English class, I got my paper handed back along with all the others except for Calpurnia Dove's. I saw her sitting at the front of the class empty-handed, biting her lips to keep from smiling, looking down at her desk so no one could see her eyes shining.

Miss Grossman had marked my paper A—. She wrote across the top of the first page: *Watch your spelling. But this is excellent. You know, going away to college is a way of traveling. You see a lot and you're getting your first taste of independence, and you're on your own. Did you ever think of that, Little Little?*

Miss Grossman was the only person I knew who'd figured out a way of going to heaven without dying. You just went from high school to college.

If you were accepted by a college, Miss Grossman put your name up on her bulletin board with a gold star pasted next to it. You got a silver star for even sending in an application.

My father always told me, "It isn't wrong to want to skip college. Just be sure you're not passing it up for the wrong reason."

"Just be sure," my mother'd chime in, "you're not trying to avoid the real world."

"Of course I'm trying to avoid it," I told her. "It's real to you, but not to me."

"There's no way to avoid the real world," my father could be counted on to point out in these conversations. "Not going to college is not going to stop the real world from being right outside the front door."

"Then I'll stay in the house," I'd mutter back.

On and on.

Cowboy always said our mother faced the real world the same way someone handled a headache: she took something for it, from a bottle.

After we got our stories back and all read Miss Grossman's comments, she said, "And now I'd like to read something for you that Calpurnia Dove wrote."

It began:

30

The first time I was ever called nigger I was four years old and went home crying. Didn't even know why I was, didn't even know what "nigger" meant. Only knew it was bad. So my mother say oh they got around to saying that to you, did they, well get in the boat here along with the rest of us, you got a lot of company on the stormy sea, honey, ain't one of us not been called that, ain't one of us heard "nigger" for the last time, either.

I used to daydream that I was from an all-dwarf family. I would imagine my mother, father, grandparents, and Cowboy all shrunk to my size, living in a little house locked in against a larger world, laughing at them and cursing them, sharing their tyranny with other La Belles.

Although in various ways and straight out I was told by my mother I would not grow to be as tall as other people, it did not sink in until my little sister grew bigger than I was.

In every room of our house, there is a chair my size.

When Cowboy was very young, she would always try to sit in my chairs. For a time, my father added other small chairs to appease Cowboy, until she was too big to be comfortable in them.

When she stopped sitting in the little chairs around the house, I grabbed at them ecstatically, as though they were cake and the other hungry cake-eater in the house had suddenly dropped out of the contest.

Then came the day Cowboy no longer needed to be lifted to the drinking fountain outside Lathrop's on Main Street, and no longer needed to stand on the box to wash her hands in the bathroom sink.

The picture was coming into focus.

My mother answered all my questions in tears, and my father never gave up the idea of measuring me by the long yellow tape measure fixed to the kitchen wall.

Cowboy, during that period, let me have things of hers she really wanted for herself.

When school let out that Friday afternoon, it was like a summer day and I took a walk in Stardust Park.

When I saw him outside the penny arcade, I thought he might be someone we'd invited to my party, who'd arrived a day early.

I took a good look at him. My mother'd describe him as "not p.f.," which was her way of saying someone was not "perfectly formed."

That morning, at breakfast, my mother'd said, "We have all p.f.'s coming to your party except for Jarvis Allen and Lydia Schwartz, and neither one of them bothers me. They're both from lovely families and Lydia's so cheerful about her little lame leg. . . . Jarvis plans to study law, which I told your father is remarkable."

"What's remarkable about it?" I said.

"He'll be getting down all those heavy books," my mother said.

"Law books, Little Little," said my father.

"He's going to be a lawyer like his father," said my mother. "They'll be Allen & Son."

"He's setting a fine example," said my father.

Whoever the dwarf was in Stardust Park, he wasn't Jarvis Allen or Lydia Schwartz.

I walked in the other direction, thinking of Calpurnia Dove's boat on the stormy sea, wondering why I went the other way and not toward him.

He made me think in those few seconds of Gnomeland.

It was in the park for only one summer.

That was the summer I was twelve, and it was the only summer my parents did not take Cowboy and me to the park.

I remember one night at the beginning of the summer, overhearing my father and my grandfather.

"She's got to see her own kind someday, Larry," my grandfather said.

"Not that way," my father said. "Not on exhibit like freaks."

"I agree, but—"

"But *what!*" and my father's voice was raised and angry. "I want them out of there! How did they get in there in the first place?"

The next year they were gone.

I had the feeling the dwarf in the park was following me, and I decided if he was, I'd wait for him. I'd speak to him. I looked back once and he was standing by the roller coaster.

I realized I was relieved. I always was timid when it came to meeting anyone new.

But I did glance back a second time, and watched, astonished, while he did a cartwheel, and then, on his feet, gave me a lavish bow.

I laughed out loud but doubted that he saw or heard it from that distance.

That same summer Gnomeland was at Stardust Park, my grandfather took me to Pennsylvania.

We were approaching a motel and I was seated beside him in his black Lincoln, strapped to my kiddyride, about to have a "surprise"—his only explanation for this weekend trip in the dead of August.

My grandfather, Reverend Warren La Belle, is a cream puff whose soft sweet center isn't immediately visible. If you know him, you know it's there, but he is a big man with craggy features and bushy eyebrows, who barks out his sermons and frowns his way through most days.

He isn't a man you question about a surprise he's planned, and I didn't ask any questions as we took that unusual journey together.

The first thing I saw was a red-white-and-blue banner over the coned roof of The Pennsylvania Dutch Inn, saying:
WELCOME TADpoles AND PODs!

"What are 'TADpoles and PODs,' Grandfather?" I finally ventured. We were driving up a circular road, heading toward the parking space behind the motel.

"You'll see, Little Little."

Then, coming into view, coming out of cars and around the sides of cars, falling from the heavens for all I knew, were others like me, redheaded, blond, blue-eyed, brown-eyed, straight, twisted, beautiful, ugly, in-between: a world of me.

My grandfather parked and turned off the ignition. "We're at a convention, Little Little. 'TAD' stands for 'The American Diminutives,' and TADpoles are the children."

"And 'PODs'?"

"Parents Of Diminutives." He looked down at me, watching me watch out the car window.

"Where did they all come from?" I said.

"Their homes. Same as you."

Then he put his hand over mine. "Your mother and your father were against this, Little Little. You know how they are where you're concerned. They'd keep you under glass, if they could, to protect you. Your mother, particularly. She's afraid you'll see others who aren't in as good shape as you are and it'll upset you. Well, I see people my size lame and twisted, too, and so should you. This isn't a perfect world, Little Little, far from it. We're all mixed in together. Right now you've got the world in miniature, in more ways than one. Want to have a look?"

The pool at the motel had been drained of most of its water, since the only guests that weekend were TADpoles and PODs. The deep end was only about four feet, and the shallow end one foot.

My grandfather made himself at home with the PODs after I changed into my bathing suit. I could hear him behind me, up on the lawn, his deep voice pontificating and his laughter thundering louder than anyone's.

I looked around shyly and finally spotted a girl playing with a large red rubber ball, in the water by the swimming-pool ladder, down at the deep end. She was a most amazing-looking girl with the kind of gossamer blond hair angels have, perfect skin tanned from the sun, and dancing dark eyes that flashed with her wide, white smile.

I was as vain about my swimming as I was about my own blond hair, which was longer than hers and straight, not curly like hers. I swam vigorously toward her with my best strokes, then grabbed hold of the side and took off my cap, tossing my hair.

When I told her my name, she said, "If you're going to swim, you have to wear your cap. It's a rule."

"Well, I'll just hold on here for a while. I'm from New York."

"Your hair is touching the water."

"It always gets a little wet anyway."

"It shouldn't touch the water. It's against the rules."

"What's your name?" I asked.

"My hair isn't touching the water because I can stand at this end," she answered.

We looked at each other for a moment, and I heard the

shouts of the other kids and the soft rock being pumped through the loudspeakers. I saw her dark eyes hardening ever so slightly although the smile stayed on her mouth.

"Maybe I should get out and put my cap back on," I said.

"I'd say so." She moved out of my way so I could climb the ladder.

As I reached for the rung she said, "I'm four foot one. I can stand at this end."

She wasn't finished.

"You'd better not swim down at this end if you can't touch bottom."

"I'm a good swimmer."

"But I'm really not one of you," she said. "You'd better go meet the others."

She was the first one like me I'd ever talked to.

Later, as I made friends with the others, they told me her name was Eloise Ficklin, and she never made friends with TADpoles who were perfectly formed.

"She's a repudiator, that's what we call her kind."

"I call her mean."

"She hates coming to these conventions but her parents make her come. She wants to pass, to pretend she's just short, so she picks out TADpoles who aren't like her at all, and claims she's helping out. The more you're like her, the less she'll like you."

My grandfather said to me that night, "Well, you have learned something about prejudice today, Little Little. The person at the top of the ladder doesn't pick on the one way at the bottom. He picks on the one on the rung next to him. The fellow way at the bottom picks on the fellow on the ground. There's always someone to look down on, if looking down on someone is your style."

"I really hate her," I said. "No one's ever treated me that way, and I'd never treat anyone that way."

"Oh, you may get around to it," my grandfather said. "No one looks up all the time. When things get tough, your eyes drop, Little Little. Just remember to raise them back up before you've lost your direction."

"What about having an enemy? Is that looking down on someone?"

"Enemies you look square in the eye, as you do friends. You don't make too much of them or too little. You see them for what they are."

"Then Eloise Ficklin is my first enemy."

"Sounds like you made a good choice," my grandfather said.

That night I prayed for God to get Eloise Ficklin. But if He did, He didn't do any permanent damage.

Eloise Ficklin now stars on television as Dora, The Dancing Lettuce Leaf, in the commercial for Melody Mayonnaise.

Sydney Cinnamon 5

At Twin Oaks, after you finished grade school on the grounds, you were mainstreamed to Wilton High School.

That was where I met Coach Korn and Digger Starr.

Before I worked up my act as The Roach, and became the mascot of the Wilton Bombers, I would hang around the football field on fall afternoons.

Every September, Coach Korn would say the same thing to prospective team members.

"Suppose I tell you to run into a brick wall. If you run through it, you're a fullback. If you bounce back, you're a halfback. If you stop and walk around it, you're a quarterback!"

Digger was a fullback, a freshman when I met him. He was a lovesick fourteen-year-old, big and blond, and mean when he was drinking beer. What Digger remembered most about me from those days was that I became The

Roach, and fans came to the game as much to see me perform at halftime as to see The Bombers play.

What I remembered about Digger was an afternoon in Sip-A-Soda, in Wilton, when he got mad at me for telling him not to open a can of beer in there or we'd get tossed out. Digger lifted me up and carried me back to the storeroom. He set me on a high shelf next to gallons of Coke syrup. I was there three hours until the manager found me and helped me down.

But there were happier times, too, when I was tagging after Digger, feeling protected by him, cruising by Laura Gwen's house with him in his car, listening to his confidences about her, which always began, "Sydney, you're the only one I'd ever tell this to and I'll break your tiny neck if you tell anyone else!"

We had been pals enough for me to want to see him again.

That Friday night we all ate Chinese food in the front of the trailer, Stouffer's Beef Chop Suey with Rice, boiled up in the plastic pouches by Laura Gwen.

I was catching up on their news while we sat in front of the TV, hoping as always for a glimpse of Dora, The Dancing Lettuce Leaf.

Laura Gwen had put on weight the same as Digger, but you could see distant traces of the pretty cheerleader she'd been. She still had the same dimpled face and soft blond curly hair, light green eyes looking a little more tired that night. She snapped at Digger for calling me "Roach."

I told her I didn't mind it.

"Well, I mind it. I would hate to be called Roach."

"Why? They've been around 300 million years, so they're survivors."

"They're filthy things!" Laura Gwen said.

"They aren't. People are," I said. "Roaches drag people's dirt around, not their own."

"Can we eat this here chop suey without talking about roaches?" Digger complained.

"Then don't call him Roach. Call him Sydney," Laura Gwen said.

The twin babies (the reason they'd had to get married) in the two big laundry baskets in the kitchen were testing out the idea of crying. One would go "Ant ant" and the other'd go "Ant ant ant." But they weren't into it wholeheartedly yet.

"Do you know the preacher Little Lion, Sydney?" Laura Gwen asked me.

"He's a midget, too," Digger said.

"I call myself a dwarf," I said. "What about him?"

"He's coming to La Belle this Sunday," said Laura Gwen. "One of the reasons we brought the trailer over is to stay so we can see him."

"One of the reasons *you* decided we'd bring the trailer is to stay and see him," Digger said. He took a swallow of beer.

"You like him, too, Digger. Tell Sydney about the time we saw him on *The Powerful Hour* on TV."

"He was testifying on *The Powerful Hour*," said Digger. "That's all."

"Which is one of my favorite TV shows," said Laura Gwen. "I had an aunt who got cured of carbuncles watching that show. She turned it on with them, and turned it off without them."

"Your Aunt Mildred is a hypochondriac, is what she is," said Digger.

While they argued back and forth about Laura Gwen's aunt, I remembered a time this evangelist came to a park outside Wilton, and some of us from Mistakes went to see him. Wheels Potter was with us, and he pushed himself on his board down to the front so he could see.

The evangelist was asking people to testify as to what the Lord had done for them. People began getting up and shouting out they'd been changed or cured or transformed overnight. Then there was a lull in the proceedings . . . then Wheels' voice. He raised himself as high as he could on his board, and he yelled, "You was asking what the Lord done for me! So I'll tell you! He just blamed near ruint me!"

I wasn't religious, though I'd been known to pray in times of crisis. Once, at a Fourth of July parade when I was dressed as a Revolutionary soldier, carrying a ten-inch rubber sword, a bulldog, who'd decided I was a walking Gaines-burger, tackled me during a rousing rendition of "Halls of Montezuma." While the bulldog chewed his way through my sword, toward me, I prayed and prayed. But prayer was not a regular part of my routine.

The twins were working up their act while Digger and Laura Gwen argued about her Aunt Mildred. They were taking turns going "Unt ant waaa unt."

There was a tire commercial on TV, no sign of Dora yet.

"We should have some soy sauce for this stuff," Laura Gwen said.

"Well, we don't have no soy sauce," said Digger.

"It goes good with it."

"There's too much salt in soy sauce," said Digger.

The babies were *ant-ant*ing in unison.

"Chop suey without soy sauce is like french fries without ketchup," said Laura Gwen, yelling over the *ant*ing.

"Then get some soy sauce next time!" Digger shouted back.

"*You* do the shopping, Digger!"

"I get what's on the list!"

"You get a lot that's not on the list, too, like beer!"

I decided to get out of their way and carried my plate to the kitchen. I stood on tiptoe to place it on the counter.

"See if they've got their pacifiers, Sydney," Laura Gwen shouted at me.

I leaned down and tried to get them to take the rubber doughnuts in their baskets and the babies let go piercing screams, their little faces the color of lobsters. I jumped back.

"I scared them, I guess," I said.

43

No one could hear me above their wailing. They looked like their little blue veins were going to pop through their skin.

Laura Gwen came strolling into the kitchen.

"I scared them, I guess," I said.

"They don't know the difference," she said.

But I was always wary of kids, even that little. Kids were always trouble. I would rather pass a barking dog on a street than little kids. In any town, little kids were the ones who knew who was off, who was crazy or different or bad, and liked to follow behind you in a line saying mean things.

I'd been followed by these little monsters my own size crying, "Bump back humpback!"—marching to it, *bumpety bump back, bumpety humpback,* holding their knuckles to their mouths to imitate horns, parading behind me like the circus had come to town.

I pulled the chair over to the sink, ready to get up on it and help with the dinner dishes, but Laura Gwen said never mind, there wasn't room.

"Just rinse your plate, Sydney."

Digger was in there with his eyes glued to a rerun of *The Odd Couple.*

Laura Gwen was bent over the baskets calming her daughters.

It was then that I saw the poster propped behind the kitchen faucets.

THE LION IS COME UP FROM HIS THICKET

Jeremiah 4:7

LITTLE LION

appearing
Sunday, September 27, 9 A.M.
First Presbyterian Church
La Belle, New York

"Walk with me."—*Little Lion*

Smiling down at me from the center of the poster, in a white suit with a tiny Bible open in the palm of one hand, was Opportunity Knox!

What I do after school and on weekends is drive around in my car.

It was my sixteenth-birthday present, ordered for me by my father, equipped with extension pedals.

My father says his first car was blue, too, an English Ford he called The Love Bug. My mother says oh yes and wouldn't you still like to drive around in it with Lana Waite, and watch the tires pop, she's such an elephant.

My mother's always teasing him about his high school sweetheart, whom we see waddling around Cayuta, her pudgy hands feeding herself maple creams from Fanny Farmer while she does her errands.

Before my father met my mother in college, he was the Golden Boy of La Belle, New York, voted "most handsome" in his class and "most likely to succeed." He has a thick scrapbook bulging with snapshots of himself. There he is in his green-and-white football uniform running for a touchdown, and there he is on the steps of my grandfather's church, Easter Sunday, in his new gray flannel suit. He is poised on the diving board at Cayuta Lake Yacht Club a moment before he performs one of his super swan dives, and all in white he steps aboard his sailboat to win another race. All the teenage poses, including those with Mrs. Waite when she was young and slender, the pair of them off for a picnic on bicycles, off to the school prom in formal clothes, off to ski, to skate, The Ones at La Belle High School in their day.

I look at those old photographs and imagine some sadistic oracle sweeping down on them during some golden moment, telling her she'll end up so fat she'll break chairs, and him he'll father the town dwarf.

My mother was also Someone in her small town, a cheerleader and all-A student who dreamed of becoming a writer and everyone said looked like the movie star Grace Kelly. But in La Belle, New York, she was the outsider, and there were those who said Larry La Belle's life took a complete turnaround because he married her.

So my mother always took pains to point out Lana Waite, and say, "Look, Larry, there's your old girl friend, Orca the Whale!"

I go to La Belle High with Wendy Waite, her daughter, who is the school fatty and one of the ones I give rides to after school. I pick my passengers carefully, although there are no lines in the school parking lot waiting for the oppor-

47

tunity to ride with me. Calpurnia Dove, my great rival, is one of my passengers, and Gerald Percy, the town sissy, darts past the jocks who call him "fag" to slide in beside me. I even give a lift at times to Dorsey Bobbin, who shows himself to girls summers in Puck Park behind the rose-bushes until the police come, although in my backseat he huddles in a corner and says only, "Here's my street," when we come to it.

None of them are my friends, really. I don't make friends, or like to go to other people's homes where nothing is my size and everything is out of reach. In the halls at school and at lunch I pal around with Cowboy, and now with Mock Hiroyuki, who clings to Cowboy like Saran Wrap to your fingers, and says the letter *l* like *r*, so calls me "Riddre Riddre."

After school, Cowboy reports to the gym, for her only moments as a school heroine, the tallest girl on the La Belle High basketball team. Mock waits just outside the gym door for her, composing haiku ("After I am dead / Come and cry over my tomb / Little cuckoo bird").

When I've dropped everyone off at their corners, I hang out in my car. It is like my own little apartment on wheels. I have my own library in it. I have sweaters, a raincoat, extra shoes, lots of Flairs in various colors of ink, my 3-subject notebook in which I write my stories, my glass globe of the world filled with dimes all the way to the Great Lakes, and a carton full of tapes: top ten, rock, golden oldies.

What I do a lot is drive around this town.

48

They all know me in this town.

I don't know all of them, but they all know me.

They know my name and they tell the story about my father bringing his new bride back from college. They say what a handsome young couple they were, and how they built their new home on four acres of old La Belle land up on the side of Cayuta Lake called the Gold Coast, because so many of the rich in the town settled there. They describe the parties the young Larry La Belles threw, and how the moonlight sailing races started off from the yacht club, went the distance of the long lake, and wound up at the La Belle dock, festooned with brightly colored lanterns, music playing, a dance waiting, and a midnight buffet.

Oh, they were the special ones, they say, and then this beautiful blond little girl was born, as normal-looking in the beginning as any one of our children.

On and on.

People are not afraid of me the way they are of Willie Moat, who's both crippled and crazy and calls out filthy words from his bedroom window on South Street. And they aren't embarrassed to look at me, as they are when they see old Dr. Kimbrough's widow lurching around town drunk, picking through city trash baskets with three hats on her head, and hundred-dollar bills tucked in her gloves she asks the bus driver to change.

I am as different as they are, but people smile at me. Just seeing me makes them smile, the way you smile at an amusing child.

I go someplace like Stardustburger, at the head of the lake near Stardust Park, and they all know my name, although I don't know theirs. I go there a lot because I don't have to get out of my car to be served.

I read and eat and sometimes smoke a cigarette.

And sometimes someone will shout at me from another car or truck, something like, "Hey, Little Little, aren't you afraid that cigarette will stunt your growth?"

I give them the finger, the gesture my mother says she'd like to know where I learned and wishes I would please stop using.

"I'll stop when they stop with their cracks," I tell her.

"But they aren't shouting obscenities at you, Little Little."

"They aren't shouting have a nice day, either."

"Can't you just stick your tongue out at them?" my mother asks.

"Shake your fist at them," my father suggests.

"Just make a face," says my mother.

"Hold your nose as though you smelled something bad"—my father.

"Raise one eyebrow"—my mother. "You know how to arch your eyebrow?"

I give them the finger.

La Belle is a town with a problem just the opposite of mine. It looks good on the outside but it isn't that way inside.

You drive into this town and you think it's picture-postcard perfect. You see the blue lake over the rolling green hill leading into it, and you see all the old-fashioned wooden houses with front porches and third stories, tall old trees on the lush green lawns, and quaint white churches with steeples that chime the hour.

At the tower of my grandfather's church a carillon plays "God Bless America" at noon, "Old McDonald" at six o'clock, and assorted carols at Christmas.

There's an old red-brick courthouse behind Puck Park with its pond of swans and ducks swimming around, and a gleaming white city hall with marble steps leading up to six white columns.

There are elaborate modern high schools, the Super-Duper markets, the four-in-one cinema, The Soda Shoppe, all here and all in danger of becoming extinct.

For the thing that keeps new industry from moving to La Belle and makes La Belle most strange is Cayuta Prison. It sits in the center of the town, with a high wall around it and gun-carrying guards posted in towers at four sides.

My grandfather says it is like a boil on the rear end of a beautiful lady, although that's one opinion he's never shouted from the pulpit.

At first when the Japanese trap plant moved here, every-one went bananas over La Belle's good luck in getting it.

Then the Chamber of Commerce began wondering how it could sell the town to other heads of industry when all they saw on the bus to La Belle were Japanese businessmen and men manacled to other men.

The Chamber of Commerce began complaining that La Belle no longer looked like an all-American typical small town.

Little did they dream what was in store for them that would cloud the picture even more.

Last spring, after a long winter of my mother staging horrible parties where I was to make friends with my classmates from La Belle High, my mother sat me down for a talk.

"Well, Little Little," she said, "I am ready to admit I have been going at this thing all wrong. If I was a big person in a world of little people, I myself might be reluctant to try making friends with them, although I think I would have made some effort."

"I don't need friends," I said.

"Oh, honey, there's where you're wrong. Your father and Cowboy and I aren't going to be around forever, you know, and anyway you have to have a life, sweetheart. Someday get married, someday have children."

"Why?" I said.

"I just told you *why*. Your father and I and Cowboy aren't going to be around forever is why. Then what happens to you?"

"I'll get along," I said.

"Well, I'm not going to spend my days and nights worrying that you might not," my mother said, "so I am joining

POD. Little Little, we're going to lick this thing, beginning this summer. We're going to open our house to the TAD-poles and you are going to make yourself some real friends!"

There is no arguing with my mother, once her mind is made up.

From Memorial Day through Labor Day, "diminutives" began pouring into La Belle, crowding onto the bus from Syracuse with the Japanese businessmen and the convicts. The Howard Johnson motel was overrun with them, and at Cayuta Lake Yacht Club, which is across from where we live on the lake, members and guests relaxing on the lawn looked out at gangs of TADpoles jumping off our raft, crawling around our sailboats, paddling our canoes, running down our beach front, and sunning themselves atop rocks protruding from the water.

We have nothing against the little people, the head of the Chamber of Commerce wrote in an appeal to my grandfather, *but you can see, can't you, that their presence in our midst confuses heads of industry as they size up La Belle as an ideal, average small town in which to raise their families?*

There is nothing, Reverend La Belle, that we can do about the prison, and we dearly need the Twinkle Traps factory to survive. Would it be possible for Mrs. La Belle to curtail, or halt altogether, her participation in this particular organization's activities?

My grandfather responded with a demand for suitable facilities for "La Belle's new and most welcome visitors," insisting that in some convenient downtown area there should be a scaled-down drinking fountain, urinals, and telephone booth.

On his sermon board outside the First Presbyterian Church there was a message reading: *Welcome to The American Diminutives and TADpoles and PODs. . . . "See that ye love one another with a pure heart fervently." New Testament: I Peter 1:22.*

Cowboy knew my plans.

"They're very Japanese," she said.

"My plans aren't Japanese, they're just my plans."

"They're Japanese. Marrying someone you hardly know."

"I've been writing to him since last July," I said. "You just have Japanese on the brain." We were talking about Knox Lionel, a young preacher known as "Little Lion," whom Grandfather La Belle had invited to Cayuta last summer.

"You don't know what he'll be like."

"Mommy says you never know what a man's really like until *after* you've married him."

"Mommy just wants you to get safely married."

"Or just married," I said.

"She worries too much about you, Little Little."

We were in our room discussing this, the morning of the Boots/Bombers game, my birthday weekend. None of my guests would arrive before late afternoon.

At one time Cowboy and I had separate rooms, our parents operating on some theory we needed separate identities, as though we could ever confuse ourselves. But our parents try. They would fry up Brillo pads and eat them salted if they thought it would help anything. So at one time I was in my little dollhouse room with everything in miniature, and Cowboy was across the hall with her baseball bat, basketball, bowling ball, golf clubs, and tennis racquet jammed into her closet, and we'd visit.

It was our own idea to move in together. My little things are on one side of the room—the neat side—and her big things and big mess are across from me.

Cowboy sank her large hands into the pockets of her jeans and paced in her Nikes, smoking a Camel.

"When do you plan to tell Mom and Dad?"

"They'll get the good news from him."

"Oh no!" Cowboy groaned. "He's actually going to ask for your wee little hand?"

"Something like that."

"I couldn't marry a Goody Two-shoes. I couldn't be a minister's wife."

My Grandfather La Belle had discovered Little Lion at a conference on Christian Views of Eschatology. Which is another way of saying death. (My mother says crossed over, or passed on. No one dies in my mother's head. They just go on to their next appointment, somewhere the living are not.)

My Grandfather La Belle immediately invited Little Lion to a TADpole party my mother gave last July Fourth.

Little Lion is nineteen, three feet five and a half inches

tall, redheaded and freckled, a catch, who proposed to me in bold script across a sheet of stationery with "WALK WITH ME"—LITTLE LION ENTERPRISES across the top:

Though you have worn my ring only two months, Little Little, my love, we must take long steps to catch up in this world— Hallelujah! I have faith enough for two and enough passion to turn your head around! I would like to announce our engagement at your big birthday celebration. I'll be coming direct from another appearance on The Powerful Hour *(wait until you see my new white double-breasted suit—it'll blow you away!). . . . Also, let me speak to your parents privately before you say anything. That's traditional. The Bible teaches (Proverbs 22:28) "Remove not the ancient landmark, which thy fathers have set." . . . How I wish my dear parents were alive to meet you! You remind me of my own sainted mother, darling one!*

Little presents began arriving, each one with a Little Lion card attached across which he would write: "Love! Hallelujah!"

Among them was a book called *Shadow of a Broken Man,* by George Chesbro. The hero of the book was Mongo, a dwarf, who was a professor of criminology and a private detective who'd once been in the circus.

"The TADpoles should read this book," Little Lion wrote. "Here's a dwarf who got out of the freak show and made something of himself!"

I kept the book in my car library, along with other books Little Lion sent. Most of them weren't novels, and nearly all of them were about overcoming obstacles.

"Doesn't he ever read anything depressing?" Cowboy

asked me once. "It'd get me down if I had to read about rising above it all the time!"

That morning in our room, Cowboy said she hoped I wasn't just talking myself into him.

"Well, isn't that what everyone wants, what last summer was all about? Getting me married?"

"Not necessarily overnight, Little Little."

"Still, that's what it was all about."

Cowboy didn't deny it.

"When Mom hears the news she'll be overjoyed," I said.

Cowboy didn't deny that, either.

"I couldn't find anybody better," I said.

"At least he's p.f.," said Cowboy. "That'll set her heart to beating."

I said, "You like Little Lion, don't you? Didn't you like him when you met him?" I weighed the possibilities of telling my sister I wasn't sure I was doing the right thing, watching an ash as long as my first finger dangle at the end of her cigarette before it fell to the rug atop other cigarette ashes. That alone didn't impress me that Cowboy had good judgment.

Cowboy said, "The Japanese consider it bad luck to shorten your last name. Did you know that, Little Little?"

I said sayonara to any heart-to-heart talk with Cowboy, and went across to my bureau for my car keys.

On my way to Stardustburger, at the beginning of Stardust Park, I saw the same dwarf I'd seen there the day before.

He was walking along by himself, head down, kicking the autumn leaves.

I drove past him slowly, wishing I had the nerve to pull over and ask him if he wanted a ride somewhere.

I remembered the way Little Lion walked. He bounced. Everything about Little Lion was buoyant. I could almost feel a charge of energy when I touched the envelopes his letters arrived in, as though an even more miniature Knox Lionel were inside, racing up and down the loops of the script. His letters were always fat ones, with little fat hearts dotting the *i*'s. His handwriting was like he was: running boldly all over the place.

Sometimes late at night I imagined us somewhere in a little house raising kids who grew larger and larger, filled with his energy, breaking the furniture as they grew, their heads crashing through the ceilings, their arms holding us over their heads, laughing. "Hallelujah!"

While I was in my car eating my Morning Muffin, I watched the dwarf go inside Stardustburger.

I saw others watching him along with me, one big truck driver whirling around with a grin, nudging another man and pointing.

The dwarf skittered through the door, not looking in any direction but straight down.

He didn't see me, I don't think, but I decided to send him some sign that I was around, that he wasn't the only one that morning.

Sydney Cinnamon

After I woke up in The Stardust Inn, I stood on a chair by the window and looked out at the lake, and what seemed like the beginning of another hot September day.

The heat from the lights in a TV studio was nothing compared to the heat of the sun under my shell, when I was performing out in the open. My commercials took less time to shoot, too, and I didn't use up that much energy.

I hadn't done my halftime act for a while, and I felt that I needed some kind of warm-up, so I decided to walk down to Stardustburger for breakfast, instead of ordering it served in my room.

I didn't even have to ask where Opportunity was staying when he arrived in La Belle, but I did, and they told me at the desk he was expected sometime Sunday morning.

I left this note for him:

Dear Opportunity, Did anyone ever tell you that as Little Lion, in your white suit, you look like Pillsbury's Poppin' Fresh Dough-boy? I've come up from my thicket, too, and my little ass is also going first class. When you get in, call Room 807 for a reunion with another ex-Leprechaun. Guess who?

At Stardustburger I ordered a Morning Muffin and a Dr Pepper, after I managed to get myself up on a stool at the counter.

When the waitress brought my order, she put a paper-back book beside it.

"This was sent in to you by Little Little La Belle," she said.

"Where is she?"

"She always eats in her car . . . out there."

I whirled around on my stool in time to see a blue Volvo pull away.

"You one of those TADs?" the waitress asked me.

"What's a TAD?"

"I don't know what it stands for, but we had a whole lot of them here this past summer, invited by the La Belles. Little friends for her."

I picked up the book. It was called *Shadow of a Broken Man.*

What I liked best were the kind of books Cloud and I passed back and forth in Mistakes. I owe my reading tastes to Cloud, whose father was an alcoholic poet-in-residence at some small junior college. Cloud's mother had gone mad one Christmas and Cloud's father had written a poem about it called "No, No, Noel," published in a poetry journal. Cloud never read books about normals. He said there was always a ring of untruth in them.

We shared dog-eared books that were underlined and dirty with the marks of eager fingers, as we got others in Mistakes to read them, too.

There was *Very Special People*, by Frederick Drimmer, featuring three-legged men, dwarfs, giants, and pinheads. There was *Freaks*, by Leslie Fiedler. *The Dwarf*, by Pär Lagerkvist. *Leo and Theodore* and *The Drunks* about Siamese twins, by Donald Newlove. There was *Freaks Amour*, by Tom De Haven, and *The Geeks*, by Craig Nova. *Memoirs of a Midget*, by Walter de la Mare, and *The Elephant Man*, by Ashley Montagu.

All such books were frowned on by Miss Lake.

"We will *not* dwell on our differences from other people!" she would screech at us if she came upon one of these books. "We will emphasize our similarities, *not* our dissimilarities! It does no good to wallow in it!"

"She's a Sara Lee, so how does she know if it does good or not?" Cloud would complain.

It was Cloud who thought up the label Sara Lee for normals: Similar And Regular And Like Everyone Else.

All of those at Twin Oaks who didn't live in Mistakes were Sara Lees.

It was also Cloud who dreamed up Mistakes' own version of Academy Awards night, with little clay Frankenstein statues we called Monsters to simulate Hollywood's Oscars.

One year I won a Monster for "Least Likely to Be Adopted," and grinned and blushed my way up to the makeshift podium outside Cloud's closet, while everyone sang Cloud's song, "I Gotta Be Me and Not Sara Lee."

There was the year Wheels won a Monster for "Most Likely to Be Refused Service in a Restaurant," and Wires Kaplan won a Monster for "Most Likely to Scare Little Children."

Miss Lake detested this dark humor and would not tolerate any use in her presence of our nicknames for each other: Pill, Wires, Wheels, Gimp, and my own nickname in those days: Quasimodo, who was the hero of *The Hunchback of Notre Dame.*

Cloud was the entrepreneur of Mistakes, and once tried to rent himself out as a lucky piece upon hearing that in certain places down South people kidnapped albinos and took them home since they believed a captured one brought success. He also told me certain people said it was lucky to touch a hunchback's hump, and one Saturday afternoon positioned me outside Big Market in downtown Wilton, with a sign saying TUCH MY HUMP FOR LUCK $1. While the others from Mistakes went to see a disaster movie, Cloud and I were in business, until someone reported us to Miss Lake.

"Why would you do that to yourself, Sydney?" she complained as we all drove back to Twin Oaks in her car. "You didn't even spell 'touch' right."

"Cloud made the sign," I said, and Cloud passed me six dollars in the backseat of the car, my share in our venture. He whispered to me, "We should have charged more. We could have cleaned up."

"*Don't* call Albert 'Cloud,' Sydney," said Miss Lake. "His name is *Albert* Werman."

"I like 'Cloud,' " Cloud said. "Before I came to Twin Oaks they used to call me Albert Worm, or just plain Wormy."

"And 'touch,' " Miss Lake continued dauntlessly, "has an *o* in it."

I stayed in Stardustburger long after I'd finished my Morning Muffin and Dr Pepper, sipping coffee and reading *Shadow of a Broken Man.*

It was about a dwarf detective named Mongo.

Some of it I liked a lot. I liked the part where Mongo described how his normal brother carried him on his shoulders when Mongo was a kid, "through a tortured childhood brimming with jeers and cruel jokes."

It made me glad I'd grown up at Twin Oaks, in Mistakes.

If my mother hadn't decided to dump me when I was born, I could have wound up the only one different in some small town, and gone through what Mongo described.

The only thing I knew about being left at the orphanage

was that my mother signed me over to them. I was not even sure Cinnamon was my last name. For all I know they could have been making cinnamon buns for lunch in the kitchen at Twin Oaks when I was dropped off there, and that was how I came by the name. I wasn't even sure of the Sydney. Maybe he was the taxi driver who brought me to the door, or a groundsman who found me on the steps balled up in a blanket. No one I asked seemed to know any more than I did.

Whoever my mother was, I imagined her leaving me there in tears and never getting over it. I also added to that fantasy her death of a broken heart at an early age.

I recognize that there's a possibility this lady caught a fast cab direct from the delivery room of the hospital, dumped the brat with the hump on the doorstep, and went to the nearest roadhouse calling for a celebration: "Champagne for everybody! Whew, was that kid a creep and a half!"

But I can think what I want about this mother of mine, can't I? I can invent her out of my own imagination, which is not, I've grown to appreciate from listening to some stories about real mothers, all that big a disadvantage.

I've given my father a suitable escape route, too, pronouncing him dead before I was even born.

I read on about Mongo until I felt hungry customers coming into Stardustburger for lunch, breathing in my hair, wanting my stool at the counter.

Finally I paid up and slipped down off my stool.

I held the book under my arm tightly (it would come to

me in wondrous waves that Little Little La Belle had sent it in there to me). I didn't even mind when a little girl standing in line between her mother's legs began glaring at me. Okay, I'd give her two seconds to come out with something, but it was four, and I was almost out the door as she shouted, "Is that an elf, Ma?"

Someone else spoke up. "No, sweetheart, that's a shrimp cocktail!"

On my way to The Stardust Inn, I thought about what the waitress had said, that Little Little La Belle always ate in her car.

I hadn't thought of the idea that driving a car you could look like anyone else. It was the same in certain restaurants with long tablecloths and something under you to give you height.

Once, in Syracuse, New York, in this fancy restaurant where Mr. Palmer took me after we'd signed the contract for the commercials, a woman seated next to me on the banquette had asked me for a match.

I was sitting on a wooden crate tomato paste had been shipped in, atop a corduroy desk chair pad from the manager's office. It was a makeshift arrangement the manager apologized about; the children's seat was already in use.

The woman hadn't noticed.

"I don't smoke," I told her.

Mr. Palmer got this lopsided smile on his face and said,

"Sydney, all the waiters are busy. Why don't you go over to the hatcheck girl and get some matches for the lady?"

"Oh, I can wait for the waiter," the woman said.

"He'll be glad to get you some," Mr. Palmer said. "Sydney?"

I knew he was setting me up. I could feel my face get red.

"Please, Sydney?" Mr. Palmer gave me a wink.

Okay, so I gave in, got down off the crate, and started away from the table.

I heard the woman exclaim, "Oh my! I never—" and Mr. Palmer chuckle and tell her, "You didn't want to miss that, did you?"

When I brought the matches back to the table, the woman leaned down and accepted a light. "Well, this takes the cake!" she said, all smiles and purring. "He's just as adorable as he can be!"

"He's my new television star," said Mr. Palmer. "I'm Albert Palmer. Palmer Pest Control."

"Isn't he something," she said.

"Give her your line, Sydney," said Mr. Palmer.

I said, "My what?"

"Your line," he said. He laughed and reached down and pinched my cheek. "This little fellow plays a certain little insect which shall remain nameless in this fine restaurant. After a cloud of Palmer Pest Control repellent he says—go ahead, Sydney."

"You'll be the death of me," I said.

Mr. Palmer laughed harder and the woman clapped her

hands together with delight.

"Well, *you*"—she finally talked directly to me, instead of calling me "he"—"are as cute as a bug in a rug!"

"Speaking of bugs in rugs," Mr. Palmer said, reaching for his business card from the pocket inside his jacket, then winding up like a pitcher about to throw a ball, "my card!" slapping it down on the table.

The woman let it sit there and reached out for me with her long arm, hooking me in toward her.

"Speaking of adorable little bugs in rugs," she crooned, and leaned down in a halo of perfume to plant a wet kiss on my cheek.

Mr. Palmer chuckled. "I bet that's the first time you ever kissed a roach!"

So much for show business.

When I got back from Stardustburger, Cowboy was sitting on the floor in our solarium, next to Mock Hiroyuki, helping my mother make out place cards for my birthday banquet.

Mock Hiroyuki has thick black hair, as straight as Cowboy's is tangled, and he is much shorter than my sister. He always sits so close to her he seems like a tiny kangaroo who has tumbled out of his mother's pouch and is clinging as close as possible to her.

Because his *l*'s come out like *r*'s, he says, "harro."

He said, "Harro, Riddre Riddre."

My mother, with her thing about certain words, tried for the longest time to do something about the way the word "sit" came out of Mock Hiroyuki's mouth. The Japanese have no *si* sound; *si* becomes *shi.*

"Then just avoid the word 'sit' altogether, Mock," my

mother finally suggested. "Just say I'll take a chair over there."

"You can say I'll be seated," my father said.

"Or, I'd like to get a load off my feet," said my mother.

"How about I'd like to park my carcass?" said my father. On and on.

My mother was complaining that "with all these place cards to print out, I haven't even had time to see if my poem was printed in today's paper. Did you pick up a copy of *The Examiner*, Little Little?"

I told her there was a copy in the hall.

"And where have you been?" she said. "Driving around in your car, as usual. Oh, honey, you can't live in that car!"

"I don't."

"You do, and I know *why* you do, but Daddy didn't get you that car for you to hide in!"

Cowboy said in an aside to Mock Hiroyuki, "When she's in the car, nobody knows if she's big or little."

"*Ah, so desu-ka,*" he answered. It is the Japanese equivalent of "you don't say," and he says it every other sentence.

"Everybody in this town knows me anyway, Cowboy," I said. "I just happen to like to drive around."

"Well, Daddy didn't get that car for you to drive around in"—my mother.

"Is she supposed to fly it?" Cowboy asked.

"She is supposed to eat breakfast with the family," my mother said.

"And help us with these place cards," Cowboy said. "It's

your birthday banquet, Riddre Riddre."

"You say Riddre Riddre," Mock Hiroyuki exclaimed and slapped his palm across his mouth and kicked his legs, giggling.

My mother sighed and rolled her eyes to the ceiling and back.

She said, "There's a letter for you on the hall table, Little Little."

"From Little Lion," Cowboy said.

My mother said, "Go get the letter, sweetheart, and when you come back bring *The Examiner* with you so I can see if my poem's in it."

All through our house are little stools my mother calls "Belle's *sgabellos*," to help me reach things.

There is one in every room, all different and color coordinated to match the decor, some plain wood, one with a needlepoint cover, the kitchen one with chrome legs and a rubber top.

As I got up on the walnut stool in the hall, to reach Little Lion's letter, a cold chill went through me, imagining myself married to him. My father always said to take my time, and to remember that I didn't have to marry at all, which would start my mother off on a long harangue. "Of course you don't *have* to marry, sweetheart, no one ever said you *had* to do anything. But keep your eyes open for the right one, because it isn't easy, darling, in your situation. The best ones get snapped up right away. I remember when that dear little Blessing girl from Cleveland took her time deciding whether or not to marry that dear little Tompkins boy who was studying to be a doctor, and before she knew it he turned around and married what's-her-name who won the TADpole chess tournament every year, remember?"

"Mitzi Blessing isn't sorry she didn't marry Willard Tompkins," I said. "She's a teacher now."

"She isn't married, though," said my mother. "She's still living at home, and she's in her twenties now. A doctor doesn't come along every day of the week in TADpoles, not a medical doctor!"

"Mitzi Blessing could care less," I said.

"Well, her poor mother lies awake nights worrying about her, and I know that for a fact!"

"That's *her* problem," said my father.

"All we're talking about here is a happy life," said my mother. "A rich, full, happy life, which you are entitled to, Little Little, the same as anyone else."

"No one's saying you have to be married to be happy," said my father.

"But," said my mother, "you'll never convince me that Mitzi Blessing is happy teaching school period. There's more to life than that. There's children, your own home."

On and on.

Little Lion's letter was four pages long, typewritten front and back, with this P.S.:

Your grandfather suspects I'm going to talk to your father at

71

your birthday banquet. I think that's the reason he's arranged to
have me address his congregation while I'm in La Belle (so your
father can see me in action). He also wondered if I'd like to speak
at Twin Oaks in Wilton, where they have a special junior school
for the physically exceptional. (I can't make that, though.) He said
at one time you wanted to go there as a day student, commuting
from La Belle. There's so much I don't know about you, Little
Little, so much I'm eager to learn about my love!

"I don't want you taking a bus all the way to a school like
that," my mother used to argue whenever the subject of
Twin Oaks came up. "A school like that is for children
whose parents don't want them."

"Don't *love* them," my father said.

"Don't realize they have to live in the real world, Little
Little."

"A school like that one at Twin Oaks is where parents
send children they don't know how to deal with," said my
father. "Most of the children in that school *live* there."

"Maybe they like living there," I said. "Maybe those kids
want out."

"Out of what?" my mother said.

"Out of the real world?" my father said.

"Why not?" I said. "What's wrong with that?"

"There's no way out of the real world," my mother
said.

My father said, "It's there, Little Little."

"Not in that school."

"I don't even like the description of that school," said my

mother. "*For the physically exceptional.* Something about that description doesn't sit right with me. Two-headed people could go to that school."

"Two heads are better than one," I said.

"Little Little, this is a serious subject!" said my mother. "Most of the children in that place have been dumped there! Now, that's a strong word, but I think that's the only word for most of the children in that school. I don't want you spending your days in a depressing environment!"

One afternoon, my father and mother and I drove to Wilton for a tour of the school, which was a separate part of Twin Oaks.

"I just can't see you going there, sweetheart," my mother said all the way back in the car.

"It's not that it's a bad place," said my father.

"It's a nice enough place, but, sweetheart, some of those poor little things are so sad!"

"Don't call people 'things,' " said my father.

I said, "Don't you think people in La Belle think I'm a poor little thing?"

"No, I don't think people in La Belle think you're a poor little thing!" said my mother. "I'd like to meet anyone who thinks you're a poor little thing!"

"The point is, Little Little," said my father, "it's not the real world."

"The real world isn't real to me, anyway," I said. "What's real about a world where you can't reach the handles of doors?"

"Sweetheart, what door handles can't you reach that you really have to reach?"

"We're not talking about door handles," said my father. "We're talking about this school. Now, I frankly feel this school could be depressing, as your mother's pointed out. Some of those youngsters there are too physically exceptional."

"Not p.f. enough," my mother said.

"I'm tired of p.f.," I said. "I'm not p.f."

"You are so p.f.," said my mother. "You're little but you're p.f."

"There was a boy there on a board," my father said. "That's what we mean, Little Little."

"If you don't like going to school in La Belle," my mother said, "pick out any regular boarding school in the country, cost is no consideration, and go *there!*"

"And have my classmates' parents drive off saying, 'Did you see that poor little dwarf? It's a nice enough place but that dwarf could be depressing.' "

"In the first place you are not a dwarf," my mother said, "and in the second place little people who are p.f. don't depress anyone! They don't!"

"I'm not for the boarding school idea at all," my father said.

"Well, you won't let go!" said my mother. "Even if it's for her own good, you won't let go."

"She doesn't want to go to boarding school," my father said.

"She's never thought about it," my mother said.

"Why should she?"—my father.

There was always a point in these conversations when I began to be referred to as "she" or "her," as though I wasn't there in person, but very much there as their permanent, unsolvable problem.

If Cowboy was a cat she would carry Mock Hiroyuki like a kitten, by his neck, she was so protective of him.

When he announced he had to go home to get ready for the game that afternoon, Cowboy walked him up to Lake Road, to wait while he thumbed a ride.

Mock Hiroyuki is the closest Cowboy has ever come to playing with a doll, and their relationship made my family nervous.

When I went back to the solarium, even though Cowboy and Mock were at least a half a mile from the house, my mother whispered to me, "What is it she *sees* in that boy?"

She was sitting in the white wicker chair, thumbing through the newspaper. "How can she spend so much time with him?"

"Maybe the Hiroyukis wonder how he can spend so much time with Cowboy."

"According to your father, the Hiroyukis are too busy trying to set up something called a pachinko parlor downtown, a place full of pinball machines. Now, that's all this town needs!"

"This town is like me trying to pretend I'm tall," I said. "Why doesn't it just face the fact it's different?"

"And let pinball machines in right in the downtown?" my mother said. "Would you like to live in a town with a Japanese pinball machine parlor right across from The Soda Shoppe? I wouldn't."

Then she started in on the Hiroyukis, on a trap plant being one thing and a pachinko parlor being quite another, on give some people an inch and they take a mile, and the next thing you know there's a sukiyaki restaurant next to the pachinko parlor, and after that the geisha girls arrive.

I went and sat in my white wicker rocking chair, which is my size and has white duck pillows tied to it and faces the white duck couch where my mother moved to, to spread out the newspaper, rambling on about what the Japanese wanted to do to La Belle.

Once Cowboy and I found all the love letters my mother and father had written to each other. My father signed all of his "Always and all ways, Larry," and she enclosed poems she wrote in hers. One was called "Larry, Our Love Is Sputnik." *(Launched the same night / Reaching for outer space and finding itself a baby moon / A satellite of earth / Where other lovers wait and / Play it safe and never / Dance with stars.)*

Cowboy and I had gotten out the World Almanac to look up the date the Russians launched Sputnik, which was *before* my mother and father got married.

I often looked at my mother and tried to imagine her swept off her feet by any emotion. But I couldn't, any more than I could imagine her when she was my age and planning to be a famous poet.

In one letter my father wrote, *You'll be the brilliant lawyer's wife and I'll be the brilliant poetess' husband. Oh, Ava, my life—what a life we'll have!*

I'd think again of the Sadistic Oracle sweeping down on him as he was bent over the sheet of blue stationery that letter was written on.

"You want to know what it's really going to be like, Larry? You'll flunk your bar exam and go into the boot business. She'll write doggerel for the local paper."

I said to Cowboy, "The perfect couple about to live the perfect life. Then I came along."

"It hasn't got anything to do with you," Cowboy said. "It's growing up. If you could grow up and become something besides an adult, it wouldn't be so bad. Nothing good begins with 'adult.' There's adult, adulterate, adultery—"

And we'd laugh, but I was never totally convinced I hadn't ruined their life.

"Well, look at it this way, then," Cowboy would argue. "They ruined yours. It was the combination of the two of them that made you what you are, wasn't it? If you'd had other parents you might not be what you are." Then she'd always rush to add, "Not that what you are is bad."

My mother finally found her poem in *The Examiner*, across from an editorial urging that the city dump be cleared and made into an airport.

"Honey!" she said. "Turn the sound down a little on the

TV so I can read you my poem. They printed the one about autumn!''

I went across and stood on the stool to turn the sound down.

Then I sat on the stool and waited for her to read me her poem.

"Here goes, Little Little," she said, and her face was flushed with pleasure.

She said, "Are you ready?"

AUTUMN

God takes his paintbrush to the leaves,
Splashing them like an artist painting
Rich reds and browns and oranges across the green,
I catch them falling in my hands another year,
My senses suffused with beauty.
—Ava Hancock La Belle

"It's good, Mommy," I told her. I liked it all right, but it didn't make me jealous the way anything Calpurnia Dove wrote did.

"Now, don't exaggerate. Just tell me if it's good, as one would-be writer to another."

"It is good. I like it."

"Is it *really* good?"

"Very good."

She jumped up and ran across to me. "Oh, honey, they printed it!"

It didn't do any good, it never did, to say please put me down.

She held me, dancing around the solarium with me, planting wet kisses across my cheeks, both of us laughing, finally, me squirming, though. I smelled the mint on her breath and knew she'd had a few from the crème de menthe bottle she kept at the bottom of her white wicker yarn basket.

"We'll have a good time at the game!" she said. Then she began to sing: "We're the Boots! Toodle toot! We're the Boots of La Belle fame! We're the Boots who win the game! Toodle toot! Feel our boot!"

She danced faster, with me in her arms, jiggling me up and down the way I sometimes danced with our cat. "Toodle toot! Feel our boot!"

She put me down and knelt to be face to face with me.

"Did you like my poem, honey? Oh, I know I'm not the greatest poet in the world, but it's a nice little poem, do you really think so, Little Little?"

"I like it, Mommy."

She wiped a tear away. "Oh, why am I bawling like a baby, hmmm? I guess I'm just so happy!" That sounded so insincere, even to her, that she rushed on to babble something truer. "I'm tired, too, I guess. All these plans for your big birthday! I can't believe you'll be eighteen, honey. I was married the year after I was eighteen. I was a young bride. And we waited. Purposely. We waited to have you because we were so young and we wanted some years together, just your daddy and me. And what years they were! All the midnight sails from the yacht club ended right at our dock! Everyone came here, everyone!''

She hugged me hard.

Over her shoulder, I saw Eloise Ficklin dance across the television screen dressed as a lettuce leaf. Even with the sound turned down, I knew what she was singing: *"I'm dancing to the melody, Oh happy happy days, When I lie down I'll have a coat of golden mayonnaise!"*

Sydney Cinnamon 9

A sister of one of the Bombers' cheerleaders baby-sat for Digger and Laura Gwen while they went to the game.

About an hour before game time, they picked me up in front of The Stardust Inn, in a taxi I'd offered to pay for.

"Your shell needs dusting, Sydney," Laura Gwen said, pushing it in front with the driver.

I sat between them and Digger said, "Did you know the man who owns the La Belle Boot and Shoe factory has a midget daughter?"

"I know," I said.

"Which is the reason Little Lion is coming here on Sunday," said Laura Gwen. "There's going to be a whole convention of people like you, Sydney, coming in from all over. The driver just told us."

"It's a birthday party for Little Little La Belle," I said.

"Are you going?"

"I'm the entertainment."

"Are they paying you?" Digger asked.

"I'll get something for it."

"Well, that shell needs dusting, Sydney."

"So dust it!" Digger said. "While I'm suiting up, you get a rag and dust it for him!"

"I can dust it myself," I said.

"I'll dust it for you, Sydney," she said.

"Roach," Digger said, "me and Laura Gwen was remembering the first time we ever seen you, that Halloween at the game. You'd just started going to Wilton High, and you came to the game with some of them from Twin Oaks, remember?"

"I remember," I said. I wasn't likely to forget it. A group of us from Mistakes had gone to the high school stadium in costume. It was my first try at getting myself up as The Roach. Bighead Langhorn had put a white sheet over his body and gone as the explosion of the atom bomb, and Cloud had gone as God, his body wrapped in cellophane. Wheels had rigged himself up as a Volkswagen convertible, and Wires Kaplan went as Reddy Kilowatt.

"I remember I said you'd be a helluva mascot that day," said Digger. "You remember my saying that to you?" He reached for the can of beer between his legs and took a swallow.

"I remember," I said.

"Sydney, why don't you stand on the seat, to see," Laura Gwen said.

"Stand up here on the seat," Digger said, patting the seat.

"I can see enough."

"You can see the rate card is all you can see. Stand up here."

He gave the seat another pat and I stood up on it.

"That's better," said Digger. "I remember it was the first season The Bombers played after that year of austerity. That year was what ruined me."

"That year wasn't what ruined you," Laura Gwen said. "What you're swallowing down right now was what ruined you."

"Oh yeah? How's a scout going to recruit you if he can't see you in action?"

"No scout was recruiting *you*," Laura Gwen said.

"What about that day?" I said, trying to steer them away from another argument.

"I remember I told you you'd be a helluva mascot, and the school needed something like that to put it on the map," Digger said.

"I remember that," Laura Gwen said. "It was Digger's idea."

"Well, the band struck up 'La Cucaracha' and I just went into my dance," I said.

"And you were good," Digger said. "I said you'd be a helluva mascot."

"I know," I said.

"Just as long as you know that." Digger took a pull of his beer. He said, "What I'm getting at is we're pals, buddy.

We pals?" He held up the can as though he was making a toast.

"Pals," I agreed.

"So I was thinking, Roach, old pal—"

"*Sydney*, old pal," Laura Gwen said.

"I was thinking this is my last year at Wilton High, and I could make myself available to you, if you ever need something like a manager."

"Or an agent," said Laura Gwen. "Someone to book you into jobs."

"Fight your battles for you, buddy."

"You're part of the family, Sydney," Laura Gwen said.

"Thanks anyway," I said. "So far I'm getting along."

"But you want to do more than get along, buddy," Digger said.

"I'll think about it, thanks," I said.

"We'd see that nobody takes advantage of you, Sydney," said Laura Gwen.

"A little guy like you," said Digger, "needs a big guy to look out for him."

"You think about it, Sydney," said Laura Gwen.

"Just think about it, buddy," said Digger.

Laura Gwen said, "I'll dust your shell when we get there."

I left them by the locker room and walked over to the field. The teams were doing loosening-up drills, wind sprints, and light practice.

Coach Korn was still with the Bombers, his old self, barking out insults and orders.

I sat in the front row and watched for a while, then I took out the book about Mongo, the dwarf detective.

I read while the action went on around me.

The coach was yelling, "That pass was too soft! Zip it! Zip that ball!"

Mongo was about to rent a car while I tried to figure out how his feet were going to work the pedals of a rental car.

"You broke your pattern! You broke your pattern!" Coach Korn was barking.

The sun was that same hot one from the day before, and there was not much breeze from the lake.

The two school bands were arriving, taking their places on opposite sides of the field, tuning up.

Right around then I heard a girl's voice, "I see you got the book," and swung around and looked at her.

"Hello there," I said.

Little Little La Belle was dressed in the Boots' colors, a white skirt and a green sweater, with her sun-colored hair spilling past her shoulders.

I had to smile looking at her, sorry because I had a front tooth bigger than the others, with a filling out besides.

"I finally figured out who you are," she said. "You're The Roach."

I tried not to smile too wide. "I know who you are, too."

"Everyone knows me around here."

I looked down at her tiny feet, which were in tan boots with stiletto heels. I used to wear boots that high myself when I was at Mistakes, but my legs were bad, and boots like that gave me backaches, too.

"Thanks for the book," I remembered to say. "I'm still reading it."

"I see."

I got to my feet to see if even with those boots of hers I'd be taller. My hump made me look shorter, which was another reason I stood, and I found us eye to eye.

A tall man down on the cinder path, wearing a green sweater, called to her. "Little Little!"

"My father," she said.

I shot him a look that could kill because I didn't want her to go.

"How did you know I was The Roach?"

"I finally figured it out. I've seen your commercial. 'You'll be the death of me.' . . . Does being a roach get to you?"

"It gets to my bank account," I said, and we both laughed, and then I said, "I like it, besides." I made up my mind then and there to get that tooth capped.

"What's there to like about being a roach, besides the money?" she said.

Her father called her again and she shouted back that she was coming, so I began to talk fast. "I'm my own invention. I invented myself. All I know about myself is that I woke up one day over at Twin Oaks and they said my name was Sydney Cinnamon, which could or couldn't be my real name, and that's all I know. When I found out I was out of

86

the ordinary, a ball in a world of blocks, I decided even if they don't roll, I do. I decided to roll away, be whatever I wanted to be."

"But a roach!" and she made a face.

"Well, I decided to be something people don't like instinctively and make them like it. Something bizarre, like me." I stole a look over my shoulder at her father to gauge how long I could hold her attention. "If I'd have been something besides a roach, I'd have been an alligator or a snake. Something people look at and go 'Yeck!' just because of how it looks and not for any other reason. If I'd been a vegetable, I'd have been a piece of slimy okra."

She laughed and said, "Hey!"

"I'd have been crabgrass if I'd been a plant, or a dandelion. If I'd been a piece of mail, I'd have been a circular addressed to Occupant."

She said, "If you were a musical instrument, you'd be that tuba," as a tuba tuned up across the field from us.

"Not me, I'd be bagpipes. Bagpipes tuning up are the worst noise I know."

I was trying to think of other things to be, to keep it going, but half a dozen people were now standing near us, watching.

I gave a self-conscious pull to my sweater in back, and felt my tooth with my tongue.

"If you were a member of the weasel family, you'd be a skunk," she said.

One of the women watching us said something that

ended in "just darling together," and Little Little's father called her more insistently, and much louder. It sounded like LIT-TOE! LIT-TOE!

"I have to go," she said.

My mind raced with a plethora of answers to that one: naw, hang in here; were you planning to go over to Stardustburger after? Can we talk more later?—and when I couldn't seem to get any of them out, my mouth opened and out came, "Are you sure skunks are weasels?" . . . My face went red because that had issued forth, like a few soft raindrops squeezed out of a black thundering sky, when hard pellets of hail were called for.

She only laughed and lifted her hand to wave good-bye, while I felt a sharp sock of disappointment, watching her go.

When I went back to the locker room, I met Laura Gwen on her way out.

"Hey, Sydney?" she called over at me. "I went over your entire shell with Endust!"

Little Little La Belle

The day after I met Knox Lionel, at one of my mother's summer parties for the TADpoles, he called me at seven in the morning from the Howard Johnson's motel.

"Little Little," he said, "I have to see you right away!"

"It's dawn," I said. "It's too early."

"In Genesis it's written that Abraham rose early to stand before the Lord," he began, "and it is written there that Jacob rose early to worship the Lord. In Exodus it is written that Moses rose early to give God's message to Pharaoh, and—"

"I'm not awake, Little Lion!" I complained.

But there was no stopping him. ". . . Judges it is written that Gideon rose early to examine the fleece. Now in First Samuel it is written that Hannah and Elkanah rose early to worship God, and in Mark it is written that the Son of God rose early to . . ." On and on.

I finally agreed to meet him.

It is also written somewhere that many strokes overthrow the tallest oaks.

I picked him up in front of the motel, seated in my Kiddyride behind the wheel, while Little Lion stood beside me, close enough to get his arm across my shoulders as I drove.

I was dressed in one of my crisp white cotton numbers, made to order for me by our housekeeper, Mrs. Hootman, who washed and ironed them faithfully, clucking over them as though they were alive. "Now you're a dear little dress all pretty for our Missy."

Little Lion wore a white cotton jacket, a white shirt, and a red-and-white-striped tie, white pants, and white shoes and socks.

I wanted to drive down to the prison, because it was nearly nine and they let out convicts who had finished serving their sentences in time to catch the 9:10 bus to Syracuse. I sometimes parked across the street to watch them come through the gates, some carrying birdcages, all dressed in cheap navy blue suits and shiny new black shoes the state provided them with.

They fascinated me, and when I was younger they were the faces in my nightmares, descending on our house to kill us all in cold blood.

But Little Lion insisted he wanted to walk by the lake, so I headed for Stardust Park.

As we walked along, he held my hand tightly, and I told

him about the summer Gnomeland was in the park. "My father wouldn't let me see it," I said. "My father said those places attracted the worst kind of sleazy show-business types."

"Amen! Amen!" said Little Lion. "Very early in my ministry I came upon a similar place called Leprechaun Village. Most of the employees were dwarfs, sleazy show-biz types, your father is right!"

Later, by the lake, he removed a gold signet ring from his finger. "This ring," he said, "is a family heirloom, given to me when I was sixteen years old by my sainted mother, God rest her soul." He took my hand and placed the ring in my palm.

At that very moment, behind us, the roller coaster descended with people screaming, so Little Lion had to shout: "Little Little, there are only two things a man can't do alone, be a Christian and . . ." The cars passed around the curve, and he said softly, ". . . marry, Little Little."

Then Little Lion kissed me.

Cowboy told me once she'd let Wylie Case kiss her just to see what it was like. He groomed the horses at the stable where she rode. He kissed her with his mouth open and tried to use his tongue, so Cowboy socked him near his fly the way our father'd taught us in case a boy tried anything. Cowboy said all boys tried with their tongues, she'd heard other girls say that, but Little Lion's lips never opened until two seconds later when he stepped back. "Hallelujah!" he whispered at me. "Praise God, baby! Wow!"

The roller coaster cars came screaming out of the tunnel. I looked at the ring and saw that it said *Amoretta.*

"Who was that you were talking to, honey?" my father said.

"That was The Roach."

"That's who I thought that was," my father said.

We walked along the cinder path to the La Belle side of the stadium, past the Bomber cheerleaders, who were warming up with jumps. I was trying to think of some way to tell my father I'd just as soon not walk along holding hands, without hurting his feelings.

"I bet I'm the only seventeen-year-old girl here whose father's holding her hand," I said.

"I don't think I should ever let go of your hand, if you're going to strike up conversations with characters like that," he said, but he let go at the same time.

"He's really nice," I said.

"Nice? He's probably anything but nice. Those lower-rung show-business types are usually rather callous."

"He's not."

"He's not a high school boy, you know. He doesn't go to Wilton High."

"I know. He was in Twin Oaks, though."

"Well, I'm sorry for that," said my father, "but I thought we both felt the same about those types. They're the types who join sideshows."

"I never talked to anyone like that before," I said. "I didn't grow warts or anything because I did."

"You give a poor fellow like that the wrong idea, stepping up and being familiar with him that way," said my father.

Then I saw the whole family smack in the front row on the La Belle side, and I got myself prepared for Grandfather La Belle.

Cowboy and Mock Hiroyuki were arriving at the same time.

"Kon-nici-wa," Cowboy said.

Mock said, "Hi!"

I am not a demonstrative person. I do not reach up to hug and kiss, and I draw back when others reach down for me.

Cowboy is the same way. Cowboy never fails to wipe her mouth off with the back of her hand after a member of the family has kissed her. When she is caught in anyone's embrace, Cowboy's eyes panic like those of a small animal that suddenly has a cage lowered over its body.

But no one tries to pick up Cowboy anymore. She doesn't have to put up with the compulsion some have to sweep someone little off her feet and swing her around like a doll.

My Grandfather La Belle is the worst offender.

"Well well well well, how's my little lady?" he barked out, and there I was again, in midair, along with the flags and practice balls and balloons.

Then he set me down on the wooden bench while he turned to Cowboy and said, "Hello there." She ducked his kiss and ran with Mock to sit beside our mother.

Grandfather La Belle has trouble dealing with Cowboy. He seldom says her name when he talks to her. She is too androgynous for him. She has overstayed her time in the tomboy stage. When he visits our house he no longer goes out to the backyard with her for a game of catch, as he used to. He treats the fact she likes to discuss the plays and scores of most ball games as though that interest was like a red baby rash that should have disappeared from view long ago.

But I remain his darling.

He was ready to pick me up again when I jumped down from the bench, out of reach. He moved over and petted my coat instead, crooning, "What a treat that you came to the game with us, Little Little!"

"Who read my poem in today's *Examiner?*" my mother called out.

My grandmother turned to her and said it was lovely, just lovely, that autumn *was* exactly like God had a paintbrush in his hand.

"I wrote it in a day," my mother said.

My father said to my grandfather, "Guess who walked right up to that Roach fellow and started a conversation?"

"Riddre Riddre," Mock Hiroyuki answered my father's question without being asked it.

My father continued talking to my grandfather. "I turn my back and she's off talking to that Roach character."

"I like him," I said. "I like him a lot."

"Who read my poem in today's *Examiner?*" my mother called out.

94

Cowboy gave me a look and I gave her one. As Cowboy would put it, things were "a little minty."

My grandmother, who is willing to go along with anything, even when it means going back over the same thing, said sweetly, "It was a lovely poem, Ava, just a lovely analogy. . . . God's paintbrush and the autumn leaves."

"I wrote it in a day," my mother said.

"Congratulations!" my grandfather thundered, but he turned and frowned hard at my father.

Cowboy says I hear things out of the corner of my ears the same way people see things out of the corner of their eyes, while they're watching other things.

What I heard, while I was making small talk with Cowboy and Mock, was a mention of Little Lion between my father and grandfather.

I tuned in to this:

". . . fine young man, from a very fine family," said my grandfather.

"I think he has a case on himself," said my father.

"You don't even know him, Larry."

"You don't either."

"I know *about* him. There's not a finer young man in all of TADpole."

"Why does he wear white all the time?"

"You wore white when you were a young man."

"Not all the time."

"Well, there's nothing wrong with wearing white. What kind of an objection is that? You might say he drinks, or he smokes marijuana, or he steals, or he has a filthy mouth, and someone might listen to you, but who's going to listen to someone complain a young man wears white all the time?''

"I don't care what he wears," my father said.

"You just criticized him because he wears white all the time."

"It's no concern of mine."

"I hope Ava is, because Ava is going downhill in a hand bucket!"

"She's in her change of life," said my father.

"She's in the bottle is what she's in. She's been going through a lot these many years."

"Well, we all have."

"No, we all haven't! You've had your work. She's been the one to bear the brunt of it. . . . The best thing in the world for Ava would be to see Little Little married. Then she'd be free. Cowboy doesn't present the same problem, but Cowboy's got her things to work out, too. It'd be a blessing for Cowboy, as well."

The Bombers band marched out on the field for the pregame warm-up.

Cheerleaders followed behind, some cartwheeling, others pitching flaming batons four feet in the air and catching them.

When the band played "La Cucaracha," the cry went up for "ROACH!"

Sydney Cinnamon 11

Even though they played my theme song again and again, and began to chant ROACH! ROACH! ROACH!, I would not appear until the half. I knew I had strength for only one smashing performance on that hot Indian summer afternoon, and I saved myself until then.

But a small collection of my groupies gathered outside the gym, and as the game got under way, I went out to talk to them.

"Hey, aren't you going to watch the game?"

"We came to see *you*, Roach!"

They were a motley crew, some of them familiar by now. One tall, skinny, black-haired girl, with enormous black-frame glasses that made her small face look buglike behind them, pushed a tiny bouquet of buttercups at me, which she'd tied together with red yarn.

"I picked them myself, Roach," she said.

A boy with buck teeth handed me a small red balloon and asked me to autograph his sneaker. His sister had home-made fudge for me.

While I was signing "Good-luck wishes from The Roach!" across their pieces of paper, and asking them where they were from, what their names were, Mr. Palmer stopped by with a flashy blond on his arm. He was hurrying to the game, but he wanted to remind me we were having dinner that night with Mr. Hiroyuki. He gave my cheek a pinch, and called over his shoulder as he hurried toward the bleachers, "Remember that your appearance at the party tomorrow is a surprise! Don't shoot your mouth off to anyone!"

When it finally came time for me to go on, I had secured the bouquet of buttercups and the red balloon under my shell. Hurriedly I had scribbled whatever came to mind across a corner of a program, and tucked it inside the bouquet.

It was the second verse from "La Cucaracha," which I wrote out in Spanish (*Cuando uno quiere a una,* etc.), to make it more secret and romantic. Translated, it simply said: *When a fellow loves a maiden, And that maiden doesn't love him, It's the same as when a bald man Finds a comb upon the highway.*

My theme song was a strange song, anyway. Most people came to know that "La Cucaracha" meant "The Cock-roach," but few people knew the verses. Once at a Wilton High School assembly I sang the first verse in Spanish, as the song was written.

The principal called me into his office later and said,

"You're some kind of a smart aleck, aren't you, Cinnamon?"

"What do you mean, sir?"

"Singing about marijuana that way."

"That's the song," I said. "I didn't make up the words."

"You didn't make up *porque le falta, marihuana que fumar?*"

"That's the song," I said. "La cucaracha, la cucaracha, doesn't want to travel on Because she hasn't Oh no she hasn't Marihuana for to smoke."

I don't think he believed me. I think he thought marijuana was some new weed discovered in the seventies and couldn't possibly be referred to in a song written when he was a boy my age.

I had smoked marijuana only once, with a three-foot girl who worked at Leprechaun Village. One of her jobs was in the dining room after dinner, when she would pass from table to table wearing fairy wings and passing out chocolate mints on a silver tray. We smoked grass under the porch of the boathouse one night, watching the moon on the lake. I had heard that pot made you more romantic and I was trying to screw up the courage to kiss her, but after I smoked it, all I could think about was food, and the only thing she was curious about was whether or not someone with a hump could sleep on his back.

I told her no, not very well, it was easier on the sides or on the stomach, and we scampered hand in hand up to raid the kitchen of French pastries.

My big romance was with a normal-size girl whose parents had hired me to be BABY 1979 at a New Year's Eve party. Her name was Andrea Applebaum, and she wore braces across her front teeth that made my lips bleed after I kissed her. She told me she had a genius-level I.Q. and intended to become a Phi Beta Kappa when she went to college, and she made out a reading list for me of books even Cloud hadn't heard of, like Goethe's novella *The New Melusine,* in which a young man falls in love with a dwarf and becomes one himself in order to marry her.

We'd sneaked down to her family's rec room in the basement, where she played me tapes of old songs by The Beatles and held me in her lap, kissing my hair.

"Andrea Applebaum," I said at one point, "tell me you mean this and I'm not just an experiment."

"I don't mean anything I do," she said. "I'm having a good time, though."

I wrote her three letters after that night and she wrote me four.

Interesting that you've become The Roach, she wrote in the last letter. *I'm just reading Kafka's* The Metamorphosis, *in which a man is changed into a roachlike character and everyone shuns him. I suppose I would find him attractive. I did you. My mother keeps asking me who this Sydney Cinnamon is who writes to me. God! If she knew!*

I ran out of the energy to keep up my correspondence with Andrea Applebaum, but I am still reading the books on her list and have never since had such a good time on New Year's Eve.

* * *

Once I got the shell over my body, and the sun came
beating down, the stink of Endust almost made me upchuck.
But I danced until I thought I'd drop, and right in front of
where Little Little La Belle sat with all of her family.

I could watch her through the peepholes at the front of
my shell. She was standing in the front row of the bleachers,
clapping for me and laughing.

At the very end of my dance, I stopped in front of her.

From under my shell I stretched out my arm, my hand
holding the red balloon and the bouquet of buttercups, with
my note inside.

For a moment she just stared, a look of surprise on her
face, her tiny mouth an *0* of wonder, until she took a few
steps forward and accepted my gifts.

Then everyone cheered and applauded, and while I hob-
bled away under my shell on my poor aching feet, the band
played the old Beatles hit "I Want to Hold Your Hand."

I remembered hearing that same song standing in my
stocking feet on Andrea Applebaum's lap, smelling the Joy
perfume in her hair, and her saying, "Cinnamon and Applebaum. Put us together and we're a pie."

Little Little La Belle 12

"Little Little," said my father, "I've never told you that you had to do something, and I've never told you that you couldn't do something."

"But you're about to now," I said.

He lit a cigarette.

The Bombers had beaten the Boots 14–7.

Soon the TADpoles would be getting off the 3:30 P.M. bus from Syracuse, and making their way to The Lakeside Motel. There was to be a buffet there that evening, and then a showing of the old film *Star Wars*.

Cowboy and Mock had taken my mother home during the last quarter of the game, in my father's car. She'd fallen asleep against Grandfather La Belle's shoulder, after a severe attack of hiccups.

I was dropping my father off at La Belle Shoe and Boot, Inc., where he planned to do some last-minute weekend work, before the festivities started.

My father drew his long legs up as he sat beside me in the front of the Volvo, his leather briefcase across his lap. He inhaled his Camel, exhaled, inhaled, exhaled, and finally said, "I'm not *about* to *tell* you anything. You'll be eighteen years old tomorrow. I've gone this long without telling you what to do, and I'm not going to start in at a point when you no longer have to listen to an adult."

"*But?*"

"But I'd like to suggest that you divest yourself of this sudden fascination with The Roach."

"I'm not fascinated by him, Daddy. I just like him."

"You're sorry for the fellow, Little Little."

"I'm not sorry for him at all. I'd like him to come to my party."

"I think if you examine your feelings closely, you'll see you're sorry for the fellow. Oh, he made a nice little gesture with the bouquet of buttercups, the balloon (I told you that a fellow like that would get the wrong idea if you talked to him), but you owe him nothing, not even sympathy."

"He doesn't even *need* my sympathy," I said. "He's a survivor."

"Little Little, when you talk about survivors, you're talking about being sympathetic. We're all survivors, but those people you have to label survivors are usually people with strikes against them: dope addicts, alcoholics, him with his hump. . . . Little Little, slow down, I'd like to live to be forty-five, speaking of surviving."

"I don't even see his hump," I said. "I talked to him and I didn't even see his hump."

"Then you'd better make an appointment with Dr. Baird for eyeglasses."

"You're talking the way Mother talks," I said. "P.f. this and p.f. that."

"It hasn't got anything to do with that. A person who goes around impersonating a cockroach has got to expect to be stamped on. If I tried to do business for LBSB and took the name Mr. Stupid, I'd have to face the fact the odds wouldn't be overwhelmingly in my favor that people would seek out my advice, or be eager to deal with me. . . . Your Roach has set himself up."

"If you're a ball in a world of blocks," I said, "you shouldn't keep from rolling, just because the blocks can't. You should roll all over the place. So he's different. Instead of trying to be like everyone else, he celebrates being different. He dramatizes it."

My father said, "Well, what I say is if you're a ball in a world of blocks, there's no sense choosing to be a spitball. Why choose to be something offensive?"

"God made cockroaches," I said, "so they must not have offended Him."

"God's not around to say," said my father. "I'm talking about how people feel. I'm talking about most people."

"The Roach and I aren't in that category," I said.

"You and The Roach aren't in the same category, either."

"I'm closer to his category than I am to yours, and to most people's. I'm only a hump away from his category."

"Little Little," said my father, "it is not the hump. Now, I'm *not* your mother talking about who's p.f. and who isn't. I'm talking about the vulgar show-biz aspects of this fellow."

"I wish he could entertain at my birthday party."

"Well, that would have to be over your mother's dead body," my father said. "What's Mr. Clean going to say about a fellow like this Roach? I thought your focus was on Mr. Clean this weekend."

"Who's Mr. Clean?"

"Mr. White Suit," my father said.

"So you don't like Little Lion either."

"I don't *dis*like him," my father said. "I just wonder why he wears white all the time."

"Ask him," I said.

We were in front of the LBSB factory.

"The truth is no one's good enough for me in your eyes," I said.

"Well, you're my sweetheart." My father chuckled. He blew a smoke ring my way and I caught it with my finger, our old game we'd played since I was a child: "Rings on your fingers and bells on your toes," he used to sing to me while he blew smoke rings, "and she will make music wherever she goes."

I pulled over to the curb and my father opened the car door. Before he got out, he turned to me. "Little Little," he said, "I love you and I want what's best for you, that's all. In my eyes, Best for You isn't having The Roach around on your birthday, and as for Mr. White Pants, I'll reserve judgment. Just don't be in too big a hurry. You drive too fast. Don't do anything too fast in life."

"The Roach was the star attraction at the game," I said.

"Well, tomorrow *you're* going to be the star attraction," said my father, getting out of the car.

I drove off thinking about the way Little Lion had begun his four-page letter to me: *Wait till you see my new suit, Babe! I had it made by the same tailor Reverend Lucky uses. Some suit! And here's something I read last night I like, written by a man who was little, too, Napoleon Bonaparte. "Great men are like meteors, which shine and consume themselves to enlighten earth." I'll be shining at you soon, Babe! Love! Hallelujah! Hallelujah!*

I remembered reading about Tom Thumb's grave in Bridgeport, Connecticut. He had commissioned a life-sized granite statue of himself to be placed on top of it, with his name spelled out in large letters, and his dates. (Over ten thousand people attended his funeral.) He had married a woman three inches shorter than he was, and when she died she was buried beside him. The words on her headstone simply said: HIS WIFE.

My favorite phone booth was the one in front of Cayuta Prison, across from the bus station. I could pull up to it, and reach the phone and the coin slot by standing on the passenger side in the front seat of my car.

While I shook some change out of my globe bank, I could
see some of the TADpoles and PODs arriving. Elaine Let-
terman, the fattest member in TADpole, was waddling to
the back of the bus for her luggage, with her mother at her
heels. Gus Gregory from New Jersey, who always dressed
as though he was from Texas, looked like a walking mushroom under his enormous ten-gallon hat as he came off the
last step of the bus. Ozzie Schwartz, the TADpole bully,
came up behind Gus and pushed his hat down over his eyes,
swatting shy three-foot-tall Norman Powers with his Pan
Am bag; on and on.

I figured out that The Roach was staying at The Stardust
Inn, since I had first seen him there in the park.

I got the number from Information.

When he answered the phone, I said, "I hated Spanish.
I nearly flunked Spanish."

"I never took it."

"So I don't know what your note says."

"Hello, Little Little."

"But thanks for the buttercups and the balloon."

"I was just resting up and reading," he said.

"What?" I said.

"I said I was just resting up and reading."

"I mean what are you reading?" I said. "Take down this
number and call me back? I'm at a pay phone."

Down the street, across from the bus station, people had
stopped to watch the arriving PODs and TADpoles.

Sydney Cinnamon   13

After I'd finished reading the book about the dwarf detective, I'd begun to read the last book on Andrea Applebaum's list, *The Obscene Bird of Night,* by José Donoso.

It was this book I described to Little Little, the story of a hunchbacked dwarf, harelipped and suffering from gargoylism, born to the wealthy Jerónimo de Azcoitia. Don Jerónimo called his son Boy and isolated him in the world of La Rinconda, a plantation he populated entirely with other monsters, so Boy would never know he was different from other people.

Then I told her about my life at Mistakes, about Sara Lees—we talked so long my ear hurt from having the phone's receiver pressed against it, and a carillon in La Belle sounded "Old McDonald."

Little Little said, "It can't be six o'clock!"

I was about to describe my summers at Leprechaun Village, but my appointment with Mr. Palmer and Mr. Hiroyuki was at seven, and Little Little said she was due somewhere a half an hour ago.

She gave me a number where I could reach her later.

"How much later?" I asked.

"Much later," she said. "Midnight."

"What about your family?"

"It's my own private number," she said. "My sister and I have a phone in our room."

As soon as I'd hung up, Digger called to invite me for another dinner at his trailer, and to complain that he'd been trying to get me for hours. I thanked him anyway and he said while I'd been yakking away the whole town was being invaded by people my size.

"If you want your shell polished or you want a ride anywhere tomorrow, call us," he said. I could hear the babies *ant*ing in the background. "We won't be leaving until after we see Little Lion."

In the bathroom, the tub faucet was built so high that I could shower under it, instead of turning on the overhead shower.

I wore a gray flannel suit I'd purchased in the boys' department at Wilton Big Store, a white button-down shirt I'd bought in the same place, and a navy-blue-and-white-striped bow tie. Then I put on my size 5 shoes and took the elevator down to the lobby, in time for my dinner appointment in the Stardust Room.

"Sydney," said Mr. Palmer, "order the sirloin steak!"

A child's seat had already been placed at the banquette

reserved for us, and I was seated in it, across the table from Mr. Hiroyuki. Although he was Japanese, he was American-educated and spoke faultless English. His son, he told me, was still struggling with the language.

"Cost is no consideration tonight, Sydney," said Mr. Palmer. "Have the steak."

My arms and back still ached from my stint as The Roach that afternoon, and I was not up to sawing my way through a steak. I ordered fish.

"Sydney," Mr. Hiroyuki said after our orders arrived, "I leave it to Mr. Palmer to tell you later all about our new product, Roach Ranches."

"Notice he said *our*, Sydney," said Mr. Palmer. "Mr. Hiroyuki and I came to a very satisfactory agreement early this evening."

"Congratulations," I said.

"But I want to talk to you about another matter," said Mr. Hiroyuki.

"How would you like to settle down in La Belle, Sydney?" said Mr. Palmer.

"How would you like to be a dragon as well as a roach?" Mr. Hiroyuki said.

While we ate dinner, Mr. Hiroyuki described a new venture he was undertaking: a pachinko parlor.

"You know, Sydney," Mr. Palmer said, "a place with pinball machines in it. They're all over Japan."

"We need a trademark," Mr. Hiroyuki said.

"The same way Palmer Pest has The Roach."

"A dragon," Mr. Hiroyuki said.

"A little dragon," said Mr. Palmer. "How's your fish, Sydney?"

"It's fine," I said.

"I think a pink dragon would be interesting," said Mr. Hiroyuki.

"The Pink Pachinko Dragon," Mr. Palmer said. "Would you like to be a dragon, Sydney?"

Mr. Palmer didn't wait for my answer. He said to Mr. Hiroyuki, "This kid got pulled out of school before he graduated. He ought to go back to school. He could go to school here in La Belle."

"A little pink dragon with smoke coming out of his nostrils," said Mr. Hiroyuki, "and this long wiggling tail."

"You want to go back to school, don't you, Sydney?" said Mr. Palmer. "This kid," he said to Mr. Hiroyuki, "reads more books in a month than I've read in a lifetime. Tell him how much you read, Sydney."

"I wish my son would read," said Mr. Hiroyuki. "Mock is too interested in television."

"This kid reads and watches television at the same time," said Mr. Palmer. "I tell him he doesn't get the full benefit of either, but who am I to tell anyone that who reads more books in a month than I've read in a lifetime?"

"La Belle isn't going to like our pachinko parlor at first," said Mr. Hiroyuki. "We need to soften the blow."

"A little pink dancing dragon ought to do it," said Mr. Palmer.

"What do you think of our idea, Sydney?" said Mr. Hiroyuki.

"I think I'd be a good dragon," I said.

"Well, you've been one hell of a good Roach, I'll tell you that," said Mr. Palmer.

I stayed with Mr. Palmer while he had an after-dinner brandy, and Mr. Hiroyuki bowed good-bye.

"Sydney," Mr. Palmer said, "Twinkle Traps and Palmer Pest are going to produce these little Roach Ranches that'll make roach pastes and roach sprays obsolete. Now, if you've finished with your pie, I'll go into it. You've finished with your pie, haven't you?"

"I'm finished," I said.

"These Roach Ranches are so effective I'm a fool to have any part in their production because they'll wipe out more roaches overnight than Palmer Pest could eradicate in a month. Thank God roaches are prolific or I'd be as obsolete as my roach bombs before you could say exterminator. Smile at that blond lady across the room, Sydney, she's watching us and may want a little nightcap with us for the novelty of it."

"What *are* Roach Ranches?" I asked.

"You see that blond lady over there? Give her a wink."

I looked across at a woman with a fur-collared white sweater over her shoulders, raising her brandy snifter in a salute as Mr. Palmer raised his.

"She sees us. I'll tell the waiter we'd like her to join us," said Mr. Palmer. "Roach Ranches are plastic traps that lure the roaches inside with a powerful odor roaches can't resist. It's their last roundup, so to speak. You'd be something like a little roach cowboy. Appeal to you? Part of the time you'd be a dancing pink dragon with smoke pouring out of your nostrils and a long flaring tail, and part of the time you'd be a Roy Rogers type roach. In between the two you could get your high school diploma right here in La Belle."

Then Mr. Palmer snapped his fingers for the waiter, smiled down at me, and sang softly, "We'll be head-ing for the last round-up. Yip-pee, tie, yea!"

After the blond lady joined us, Mr. Palmer told her I was The Roach, and she kissed the top of my head and told me she worked for the La Belle library.

"This kid reads more books in a month than I've read in a lifetime," said Mr. Palmer.

She told me I should read the poems of someone named Don Marquis, who wrote as a cockroach leaving messages in the typewriter of a newspaper office.

"His roach was named archy," she said, "and there was a cat named mehitabel who was always saying wotthehell!"

"Wotthehell!" Mr. Palmer laughed and he gave me the eye, meaning he was cutting the bait; he'd handle things from that point on without me.

Little Little La Belle 14

On our way to The Lakeside Inn that night my mother said, "I feel a lot better now that I've had a rest and a hot shower, and that's why you're down in the dumps, Little Little."

"I'm not down in the dumps because you've had a rest and a hot shower," I said.

"I didn't mean you were down in the dumps because I've had a rest and a hot shower," she said. "I meant you didn't give yourself time for a rest and a hot shower, and you know that's what I meant. You're in one of your moods, honey, and if you don't slow down we'll be killed right here on Lake Drive before you reach age eighteen."

"I'm not in a mood because of that," I said.

"Not just because of that, no, but a rest and a hot shower would have helped, and I bet you would have seen to it that you had both if Little Lion was going to be here tonight."

"That's not it either," I said.

"Then what is it?"

"These TADpole meetings always remind me of New Year's Eve. You feel duty bound to have a good time. How can you have a good time if you feel duty bound to have one?"

"I don't feel duty bound to have one, and I intend to have one," my mother said. *"If* we live to get there."

I slowed down.

"Everyone's gone to a lot of trouble to get here," said my mother. "Jarvis Allen and his mother came all the way from Missouri."

"That's what I mean," I said. "I'm duty bound to have a good time because Jarvis Allen and his mother came all the way from Missouri. He's so Sara Lee sometimes I want to throw up in his hair."

"Lit-toe! Lit-toe!" my mother exclaimed. "Jarvis Allen is one of the nicest young men in TADpole or any other organization and what does 'Sara Lee' mean? Did you say Sara Lee, like Sara Lee the cake?"

"Sara Lee means Similar And Regular And Like Everyone Else."

"Jarvis *Allen?*" my mother said.

"Jarvis Allen."

"With that little twisted leg of his?"

"Twisted leg and all, he's a Sara Lee," I said.

"Well, I don't know where you got your Sara Lee theory, but I'd take it back to wherever you got it and get a better one. Jarvis Allen has overcome a great deal to become what he is, and you of all people ought to appreciate that. You ought to thank God you're p.f. and didn't have to overcome what he's had to."

"What he's become is a bore," I said. "It hasn't got anything to do with being p.f. or not p.f. A bore is a bore."

"Besides," my mother said, "I don't see anything wrong with being similar and regular and like everyone else."

"I know you don't," I said.

"Oh, Little Little, this is no way to begin your birthday weekend. Little Lion will be here tomorrow morning and you'll feel a lot better!"

I pulled into the circular drive in front of The Lakeside Motel, where there was a banner reading:

WELCOME TO THE AMERICAN DIMINUTIVES.

"I hope the silverware arrived," my mother said. "Let me off at the front door, and while you're parking the car, park that bad mood you're in."

"Okay," I said and stopped the car at the entrance.

"Okay?" she said, leaning across to give me a kiss. "Because this is your party, Birthday Girl, and I might just read my poem for everyone."

One of the conveniences The American Diminutives provided at parties and conventions was silverware scaled down to the proper size for us. When it didn't arrive, we had to use plastic forks and spoons and knives or make do with regular services, which were always too heavy and unwieldy.

Jarvis Allen's mother always set up a little booth where

she took orders for special silverware, kitchen utensils, sporting equipment, and so on, and as I came in the back door of the inn, I saw her assembling it.

"Happy Birthday a day early, Little Little," she said. "You'd better hurry. They're about to start the meeting in the ballroom!"

By the time I got there, the meeting was under way. Jarvis Allen was announcing the names of TADpoles who had been accepted at colleges around the country.

". . . Lydia Schwartz, Syracuse University!"

Applause.

"Norman Powers, Rider College!"

Applause.

"And last of all, with all due humility, yours truly has been accepted for pre-law at the University of Missouri."

Applause and cheers and whistles.

Jarvis Allen held his hand up for silence.

"And now," Jarvis Allen said, "before we commence the festivities, I would like to suggest that we all sing our TAD-pole song, which is the first one on your song sheets, and I would be delighted to start us off!"

He began tapping his good foot and humming to find the pitch, and then to the tune of "The Caissons Go Rolling Along," he began, and everyone joined in.

> *Over hill, over dale,*
> *We will hit the dusty trail,*
> *As the TADpoles go rolling along!*

In and out, hear us roar,
  Little's better, less is more!
As the TADpoles go rolling along!
And it's Hi! Hi! Hee! Diminutives are we!
Shout out your message loud and strong (one, two!)
We're all small,
  And going to have a ball,
As the TADpoles go rolling along! (Keep 'em rolling!)
As the TADpoles go rolling along!

After I said something hateful about someone, I always had the suspicion God was going to get me for it, so I made a beeline to Jarvis Allen's side after I'd filled my plate with chicken à la king from the buffet.

He was sitting with Lydia Schwartz, and both of them were discussing their college plans, over in a corner of the ballroom.

I began to feel like Lavinia Thumb, Tom Thumb's wife, with no plans to do anything but what my husband had in mind, as I listened to them, and I tried to get a picture in my mind of what Little Lion even looked like, although there were posters of him all over La Belle. I had the image on that poster registered all right, but I couldn't remember him in any other pose than that one with his hands stretched out and the Bible in his palm.

What I could see in my mind's eye was Sydney Cinnamon's lopsided grin with the snaggly tooth and light-blue eyes, and I could hear him talking to me, and hear that theme song of his, "La Cucaracha," dancing in my head.

". . . always been somewhat of an overachiever," Jarvis Allen was saying, "but they are the ones who make the waves in the world."

I remembered a day under our raft last August when Jarvis Allen told me he'd be willing to make out with me, so I'd have the experience. I told him thanks, anyway, but I wanted my first experience to lead to my second, not to discourage me from ever doing it again, and he held my head underwater for a slow count of ten.

"I want to be a newspaperwoman," Lydia Schwartz said. "My mother worked for *The New York Times* before she got married. She could have been a great reporter but she gave it all up to have a family."

"Wisely so," said Jarvis Allen.

"Why wisely so?" I chimed in.

"I wondered how long it'd take you to put in your two cents, Little Little."

"Why wisely so?" Lydia Schwartz said.

"There can be only one Pope in the Vatican," said Jarvis Allen.

"Who's talking about the Vatican?" said Lydia Schwartz. "Not this Jew."

"All right," said Jarvis Allen, "a ship can have only one captain."

"Who's talking about a ship?" I said.

"You girls know what I mean," said Jarvis. "Children need a mother. She should be there in the home, ready when they need her."

"Yawn," said Lydia Schwartz.

"Snore," I said.

"I don't know where the hell I'd be if my mother hadn't been there for me, and where would you two be?"

I could see my own mother making her way across the ballroom toward us, all smiles, fresh from the PODs' cash bar.

"Jarvis," Lydia Schwartz said, "you are a . . . a . . ."

I found the words for her. "Diminutive pig," I said.

Sometimes little lies poured out of my mother's mouth as easily as rain fell from a stormy April sky.

"Little Little was just saying to me, coming over in the car, how very much she admired you, Jarvis"—my mother, bending over us—"and how much she appreciated your coming all the way from Missouri for her birthday."

"Did you say all those nice things about me, Little Little?" Jarvis said.

I muttered something under my breath I couldn't even hear myself.

Jarvis said, "Well, in the same fine spirit of sincerity, I have to say how very much I admired the poem you just read to all of us."

My mother didn't get his sarcasm. "Why, thank you, Jarvis," she said. "I wrote it in a day. Now you all just enjoy your dinner while I get myself something to eat. Lydia, what a sweet little dress you have on. I bet your mama made it."

"My mother can't sew," Lydia answered.

Jarvis said, "They don't teach sewing in journalism

school, though they should, to females."

"Well, it's pretty as a picture," said my mother, "and now excuse me, please."

Jarvis turned to me after she'd left and said, "What did you really say about me coming over in the car?"

"Wait until we're finished eating," I said, "and I'll tell you."

Sydney Cinnamon 15

It was only nine o'clock when I strolled out of The Stardust Room, three hours until my telephone date with Little Little.

I walked around the lobby, looking for a place that sold magazines and paperback books. I always checked out the newsstands in hotels and motels because they often displayed reading material on racks that ran the length of walls. I could stand and read the titles of all except those on the top rows. In regular stores I was helpless against counters and tables I couldn't reach.

My eye caught an enormous white wicker giraffe in the window of a store called Wicker Wonderland. The giraffe was a plant holder about ten feet tall, something I would have liked shipped to my room over Palmer Pest Control in Wilton. Even though I would have to stand on a ladder to water any plant I put in it, it would be the pièce de résistance of my collection.

It was Cloud who had started me collecting giraffes. One Christmas he had presented me with a stuffed giraffe that stood four feet higher than I did. He had written on the card, "For the smallest, the tallest!" Since then I had added giraffes in all sizes, made of cotton, clay, china, wood, and leather.

Mr. Palmer had slipped me two hundred dollars at dinner. The white wicker giraffe had a price tag tied to its neck: $185. If the store had been open, I would have bought it, but there was a sign on the door saying OPEN SUN. 9–12 A.M.

While I was still searching for the newsstand, a bellboy called me.

"Mr. Cinnamon? I've been looking for you."

He handed me an envelope. "We were afraid you'd slip by us and we'd miss you."

I gave him a tip, and ripped open the envelope to find this note inside:

They told me at the desk it's you in Room 807.
I don't believe it! Come to Room 829.
Love and kisses from the Poppin' Fresh Doughboy—
Amen, Brother!

"Sydney Cinnamon!" Knox Lionel shouted when he saw me walk through the door. "You old Leprechaun, you!"

His unpacked suitcases were on the floor of the motel

room. He was standing there in blue jeans and a black turtleneck sweater, black boots on his feet, and a black cap pulled down over his red hair.

We threw our arms around each other; then he stepped back and said, "Let me look at you!"

"You look more like a thug than a minister," I said. "Where's your white suit?"

"I have to disguise myself," he said, "or I get mobbed! I've been waiting for you, Sydney. I have to move over to The Lakeside Motel. I keep a room one place and stay another—that way I don't have to fight off the Faithful!"

He picked up the phone and said, "Room 829 here. I have bags to go and I'll need a taxi."

Then he turned back to me. "I keep my car here in the lot to throw them off. Come with me? All the dwarfs in town are over at the Lakeside, and, Sydney, there are a lot of us in town!"

"I heard," I said.

"So come with me while I settle in. We'll have a drink. You're old enough to drink now, aren't you?" He didn't wait for my answer. "What are you *doing* here in La Belle?" he said. "Where the hell have you been keeping yourself? Tell me all about it! You've heard about me, I guess. Hey, Sydney, I've got a lot to tell you! Praise the Lord, it's like old times!"

On the way to The Lakeside Motel, in the back of the taxi, he told me he had a white Mercedes convertible, a ten-room house on the Palisades overlooking the George

Washington Bridge and the Hudson River, and a fiancée shorter than he was and prettier than a picture—in that order.

"And she's from a good family, too," he said, lighting up a little brown Schimmelpenninck cigar. "Her granddaddy's a *legitimate* preacher and her daddy owns this whole damn town!"

I didn't tell him I knew Little Little.

I walked around to the back of The Lakeside Motel with him, and waited for him while he left a note in her car which read: *"Don't go. I'm here. Little Lion."*

"They're all in watching a movie right now," he told me as we went through the back door of the motel. "We'll have some time to catch up—I want to hear *all* about you, boy!"—pounding me on my hump. "She doesn't expect me until tomorrow, so she's in there with the TADpoles being a proper hostess, and she's proper, Sydney, not like the ones I used to chase after when you and me were roommates. This gal's got class!"

As soon as his bags were in the room, he ordered up drinks, a double screwdriver for himself, he said, and what about me? I said I'd have orange juice, too, but I wanted the vodka on the side. I was doing some fast thinking . . . and I wasn't a drinker.

He scrambled up on the bed and settled himself against a pillow and said, "God, am I anxious to hear about you!

And don't get *me* wrong, Sydney. I may not have all the degrees (I don't have *any* of them) but I am the little lion fighting in the arena for the Lord, for sure, Sydney! My heart's in it, A to Z! Sydney, remember that Saturday night in Leprechaun Village we put on the show and I was David in the loincloth fighting that stupid dishwasher supposed to be the giant, and that dame from the audience kept pulling at my loincloth till it slipped down and I was bare-assed? OhmyGod, I'd forgotten that one!"

While he paid the waiter for our drinks, I dropped my double jigger of vodka into his screwdriver, pretending as he turned around that I'd swallowed it.

"I like it better straight," I said.

He held up his screwdriver. "Sydney, here's to you, as good as you are, and here's to me, as bad as I am. But as good as you are, and as bad as I am, I am as good as you are, as bad as I am."

We drank to that.

Then he said, "Now that I'm doing the Lord's work, I've put all those days at places like Leprechaun Village behind me. You understand that. People don't like to think their favorite preacher spent his younger years popping out of pies at stag dinners or fishing full ashtrays off dinner tables in a Leprechaun suit, so I've wiped away those days, golden as they are in my memory and yours."

"They aren't particularly golden in mine," I said.

"Well, I'm not looking down on anything we ever had to do to make a buck in this life, God knows, Sydney, and

126

I want to hear how you've been doing, but you have to understand the Lord's work is big business. I'm talking about dollars, Sydney, big bucks, and you can't get out on the wider seas of industry in the same old canoes you used for little lakes and streams."

"Does she love you?" I asked him. "Does she tell you she loves you?"

"Does who tell me she loves me? My fiancée?"

"Little Little La Belle," I said.

"She hasn't had the chance to say yes, thank you, praise God, or hallelujah, which is why I'm here and turning down the big bucks at a tent meeting my organization had scheduled in the hills of Tennessee. It's her birthday tomorrow, and we'll finalize it all tomorrow."

Then he hopped off the bed and said on his way to the telephone, "I'll have one more double order sent up for us, Sydney. I'm not a lush, believe me, but I drove the whole damn day to get here, straight from a taping of *The Powerful Hour*—I was in the testimony segment, and I'm beat, my boy, and I want nothing more than to sit back and hear about you."

His four shots combined with mine finally did him in, and near ten-thirty I helped him from the bathroom to the bed. As we waddled across the room together side by side, I saw us in the full-length mirror and thought of the Siamese twins in Vladimir Nabokov's short story "Scenes from the Life of a Double Monster," which he'd described as walking like drunken dwarfs supporting each other.

He had passed out cold on the rug before I got him up on the bed, and I put a pillow under his head, admired his soft bright red hair and freckled cherub's face, and threw a blanket over him.

A motel employee told me *Star Wars* was coming to an end, which gave me time to slip out into the parking lot and get Little Lion's note from the blue Volvo.

I was breathless from all this exertion as I posted myself just outside the door of the ballroom.

"How did *you* get here?" she said when she came out with all the others.

I was still panting like a dog. "I ran all the way."

Little Little La Belle   16

"Little Little," my mother said, "where are you? We've been worried out of our minds. Larry, pick up the den phone, it's Little Little!"

"I'm at The Palace," I said. "I'm going to see the Midnight Monster Double Header."

"It's midnight!" my mother said.

"That's when it starts," I said.

"Little Little"—my father's voice—"where are you?"

"She's at The Palace Theater," said my mother.

"It's midnight!" my father said.

"And I'm eighteen," I said.

"Happy birthday, sweetheart," my mother said, "but you know what we think of The Palace."

"What are you doing at The Palace Theater?" my father said.

"She says she's going to see the Midnight Monster Double Header," said my mother.

"I'll be home when it's over," I said. "I'm all right."

"Now just a minute," said my father. "Who are you with?"

"Are there other TADpoles with you?" said my mother.

"I'm with one," I said.

"Who?" my mother said.

"Who are you there with?" my father said.

"You promised me you'd come right home after *Star Wars*," said my mother. "How many movies can you see in one night?"

"Three," I said.

"Who are you *there* with?" my father said.

"His name is Sydney Cinnamon."

"You're there with a boy?" my father said.

"I don't know any boy named Sydney Cinnamon," said my mother.

"Is he a TADpole?" said my father.

"He's not on our list," my mother said. "I know every name on that list."

"Who is he, Little Little?" said my father.

"Is he little?" my mother said. "Is he a diminutive?"

"He's little," I said.

"Who *is* he?" said my father.

The operator broke in at that point and demanded more money for the next three minutes.

"What's the number there?" my father said.

"The show is going to start any minute, so don't call me

back," I said. "I just want you to know I'm okay."

"Where did you meet him? He's not on our list," my mother said.

"Little Little," my father said, "you're not with The Roach?"

"The *Roach?*" my mother said.

There was the operator's click and the dial tone.

I thanked Mr. Gruberg, the manager, for the chair I'd used to make the call. He knew me from all the times Cowboy and I had sneaked to the theater last summer, while my parents went to dances at Cayuta Lake Yacht Club. We only had time to see one feature without their knowing we were there. My parents didn't object to the movies The Palace showed as much as they feared the rats that were supposed to live in The Palace, and "the element" that went to the late night shows—a lot of kids who smoked pot and made out in the back rows, and some of the town drunks who dropped in to nap.

While Sydney bought us a huge container of popcorn, I lit a cigarette for a few fast puffs before we got inside.

A red-faced fellow with blurry eyes asked me where my mamma was and if she knew I was smoking cigarettes.

"This little pixie is older than you think," Mr. Gruberg told him.

"Come on," Sydney said, and we went inside, and all the way down to the front row.

The feature was beginning, *The Incredible Two-Headed Transplant*, starring Bruce Dern.

Sydney passed me some popcorn. "Did you ever see *Ghidra, the Three-Headed Monster*? He was two hundred feet tall besides."

"I saw *The Thing with Two Heads* here, last summer."

"That was boring," he said. "Ray Milland had his head grafted onto Rosie Grier's and they spent the whole time talking about racial issues."

"I know it," I said, "but it was on with *Curse of the Werewolf*, which was what we'd really gone to see, and never got to see because we could only see one and it was last."

"It was good," Sydney said. "It was about a feral creature. There's a science fiction writer called—"

People behind us went, *"Shhhhh!"*

"Philip José Farmer," Sydney whispered. "He wrote a whole anthology about feral men called *Mother Was a Lovely Beast.*"

"You read a lot of weird stuff," I whispered back.

"Shut up!" a man yelled.

"You read Sara Lee," Sydney whispered back.

We ate all the popcorn and tossed the empty container under the seat. Just as Bruce Dern began to stitch two heads onto one body, I grabbed Sydney Cinnamon's hand and said, "Operations give me the creeps."

He looked over at me and smiled, and then he said something I couldn't hear.

"What?" I whispered.

"I said I'm planning on having dental work done," he said.

132

He had his free hand across his mouth so I could hardly hear him.

"What did you say about the dentist?"

"I'm hoingtoonehoon."

"Take your hand away from your mouth I can't hear you."

"Skip it," he said.

I watched the two heads being stitched on the body as I thought about what he could mean and then I got it. "Oh," I said. "Your front tooth bothers you."

"I'm going to have my fang capped," he said.

"How very Sara Lee," I said.

He gave me a shove in my ribs with his elbow.

We sat there staring up at the huge screen, holding hands tightly, when what sounded like a herd of elephants charging down the aisle produced my father.

"Little Little, I'd like to talk to you!"

"This man is my father, Sydney."

"How do you do," said Sydney.

The people behind us began shouting at us to shut up.

"Little Little, come out into the lobby!" my father demanded.

"Daddy, we're in the middle of the movie."

"You heard me," he said, and Sydney let go of my hand.

I said to Sydney, "You don't have to come."

"I'll come," he said.

My father waited for us to get out of our seats and then followed behind us. I could see that he had on his pajama top under his overcoat, he had left our house in such a hurry.

The three of us stood in the lobby, my father crouched over with his knees bent and his hands on his knees. "It is now one in the morning. You have a big day ahead of you tomorrow, Little Little."

He didn't look in Sydney Cinnamon's direction at all.

I said, "Daddy, this is Sydney Cinnamon."

"I know who it is."

"How do you do, sir," Sydney said.

"Howdoyoudo," my father said so fast it sounded like one word, still not looking at Sydney. "Did you hear what I said, Little Little? You have a big day tomorrow, beginning very early in the morning."

"We'll only stay through the first feature," I said.

"I've come to take you home."

"Thanks, but I have my car."

"We'll pick up your car tomorrow." He finally gave Sydney Cinnamon a fast glance. "You can get a cab—there's a cab stand across the street."

"This is what I call really humiliating!" I said.

"Call it anything you want," my father said. "I'm taking you home!"

Then my father straightened up and barked out, "Lit-toe, Lit-toe, right now!"

"But—" said Sydney Cinnamon.

"Right NOW!"

"On my eighteenth birthday?" I said.

134

"Hey," Sydney smiled at me, covering his tooth with his hand. "Happy Birthday!"

He had barely finished the sentence when my father picked me up bodily and carried me out of the lobby, into the street.

"That is the last you'll see of The Roach!" he said.

Sydney Cinnamon 17

When I wake up in my room in Wilton, the first thing I see is myself reflected in the full-length mirror across the room. I am in my little bed, made especially for me by a Wilton carpenter, and next to it is the bureau he built to my size, and the desk and chair. I know the real world begins just outside my door and down the hall, where the bathroom confronts me with the toilet and sink, which take great effort to reach, and I am again like a mushroom growing in a forest inhabited by giants. But for that space between waking up and getting up, I am myself. I wiggle my toes and see them reflected at the foot of my bed, pulling the covers away from the mattress. I sit up and put a pillow behind me, and my feet stretch out a quarter of the way down my mattress.

When I am traveling and lonely, I miss my own room, and I woke up in The Stardust Inn to find my body lost in the enormous double bed, as the events of the night before came back to my consciousness. I put the huge pillow behind me and sat up, my feet coming just to the part of the sheet turned over at the top of the mattress.

I remembered Mr. Gruberg, who drove me back to the Inn so I didn't have to get a taxi. He was leaving The Palace anyway, he said, and said he had to laugh when he saw Larry La Belle just pick up his little girl and carry her off kicking and pounding with her little fists.

"Oh, no offense," he said, "I know you didn't feel so hot about it. I'd like to be able to take my own kid in hand that way, though. Well, don't worry, young fella, you are a *young* fella, aren't you. How old?"

"Seventeen," I said.

"Don't worry, because there are other fish in the sea."

"Not in my sea there aren't," I said.

"In any sea," he said emphatically.

I didn't want to chance soiling his seat, so I didn't stand on it but rode beside him watching the tops of trees and blinking traffic lights. I thought of a short story called "Godman's Master" by Margaret Laurence. It was about a dwarf who had been made to live inside a box all his life while his master pretended that inside the box was an oracle. The dwarf would make pronouncements through a hole, and sometimes he would cough, this tiny cough that sounded like a butterfly had cleared its throat. After a man rescued him from the box, he insisted to the dwarf that there was much more to freedom than just not living in a box.

The dwarf had answered, "You would not think so if you'd ever lived in a box."

"Mr. Gruberg," I said, "you and I don't swim in the same sea."

"I don't know about that," he said. "Last summer I met a lot of little people. The town was filled with them because of her, you know, she's getting to the marrying age I heard was the reason. So I observed little people pretty well. They'd come down to see the shows."

He smiled down at me. "I kept a pile of telephone books to boost them up high enough to see the screen."

I thanked him for the ride to the Inn, and walked through a lobby swarming with people, although it was two in the morning. They were some of "the Faithful" Little Lion had described to me, looking for rooms, which were scarce that weekend in La Belle, looking for a glimpse of Little Lion, crowded into the coffee shop for late-night snacks after coming off the road.

Crowds always made me nervous. My toes got stepped on and I got jostled about in them, so I hurried through the lobby to the elevator.

Just as I was standing on tiptoe to fit my key into the lock, I heard my telephone ringing. It rang insistently while I worked the key, pushed open the door with my shoulders, and tried to locate the phone in the dark. It kept ringing while I dragged the desk chair across under the light switch, and just as I got up on the seat, the telephone stopped ringing.

It could have been Mr. Palmer, Digger, Little Lion, but

I sat on the bed with my feet hanging down the side, wondering if Little Little had tried to call me.

When I finally crawled under the covers and fell asleep, I dreamed her father chased me down a winding corridor, caught me, slapped me into a box, and began pounding nails into its side.

He called at me through a hole, "Good-bye, butterfly."

"Sydney," Mr. Palmer said, "the banquet begins at four. You'll enter the ballroom at around five-fifteen with the birthday cake. The band will play your theme song right after they play 'Happy Birthday.' Sydney?"

"Yes," I said, swallowing a mouthful of toast. "I'm listening."

"I'll drive you there, and right after your performance we'll head for Wilton. Mr. Hiroyuki was crazy about you, Sydney. We had an early breakfast and he brought along a model of the Roach Ranch. . . . Do you want to go hear Little Lion with me?"

"I have something I have to do first with Digger Starr," I said. I looked at my watch. It was eight o'clock. "I have to hurry, Mr. Palmer. I'll go to church with Digger."

"I thought up a name for you, Sydney, to use in our first commercial. How does Roy Roachers sound? You'll be in chaps and a sky piece."

"What's a sky piece?"

"A cowboy hat, Sydney! They call them sky pieces in Texas. You'll have a new line. We're throwing out 'You'll be the death of me.' Instead, you'll swagger out in your chaps and sky piece, ready to draw your pistol, and you'll say: 'Name your poison!' Then 'Roach Ranch' will flash across the screen and you'll keel over. Like it?"

"It's okay," I said.

"It's dynamite, Sydney!"

" I'm in a hurry, Mr. Palmer."

"Sydney," he said, "don't be late. Have your shell down in the lobby so we can leave there at four-forty-five sharp. This is an important event where Hiroyuki's concerned, and remember to keep it secret. It's a surprise!"

"Oh, it'll be a surprise," I said.

"Maybe I'll see you in church, Sydney."

"Maybe. But we'll probably be a little late."

"Not *probably*," Digger complained when I told him the same thing down in the lobby. "We will be. Laura Gwen's already in line outside the church along with a couple dozen dwarfs. I hope this doesn't take too long, Sydney."

"I tried to get them to deliver it," I said as we walked toward Wicker Wonderland. "I talked to them on the phone but they don't have anyone to take it out to Lake Road."

The La Belles were probably already at church. I counted on that.

"You know what the cab fare's going to be? They'll soak you, Sydney."

"Cost is no object," I said, sounding like Mr. Palmer.

"We better make it to that church before Laura Gwen walks," Digger said.

"She won't walk," I said. "Where would she go?"

"That's what Little Lion calls coming to Jesus," Digger said. "He calls it walking. He yells out for people to walk with him."

Then Digger said, "What's this all about, Roach?"

"It's about a birthday present."

"Well, me and Laura Gwen are always at your service. You keep that in mind, old buddy." He grinned down at me and messed my newly combed hair with his large hand.

"Another thing," he said as we arrived at Wicker Wonderland. "That time I stuck you up on the shelf in Sip-A-Soda? I came right back to get you down, you know."

"Okay," I said. I smoothed my hair back with my hand and waited for him to open the door.

"You was already down when I came back," he said.

"After three hours I was."

He bent over to hear me better, as he opened the door. "What'd you say?"

"I said I don't hold grudges, Digger."

If I did, I didn't after Digger carried the ten-foot white wicker giraffe out to the taxi stand in front of The Stardust Inn.

Around the neck of the giraffe, he'd tied the envelope with a card inside.

I long for you, it said.

Little Little La Belle 18

"Tanoshii tanjobi, Riddre Riddre," Cowboy had whispered at me early that morning, kneeling beside my little bed in her pajamas. "That's 'Happy Birthday' in—"

"Japanese!" I finished the sentence for her and pulled my covers over my head. "Go away! I'm not speaking to anyone in this family!"

"I'm the one who shouldn't be speaking to you," she said. "I have to wear a dress today because of you!"

"Go a-way," I said. *"I* don't care what you wear!"

Name the one thing Cowboy hated most, next to not owning a horse, and it would have to be wearing a dress.

"I have to wear a dress and panty hose and pumps and go to *church!"* she said. "All because of you!"

I stayed under the covers and listened to her rattling hangers in her closet across the room. I was mad at her because of something she'd said the night before.

The first thing my father'd done when he'd brought me home was unplug the telephone in our room and take it with him.

Cowboy had held her sides laughing after he'd stormed out of the room, and then asked me what had inspired me to run off with Dwarf Longnose anyway?

That was a reference to a book that went way back to our childhood.

Cowboy had brought the book home from the library when she was around five years old. She had selected it herself, along with some others, from Kiddy Corner, telling my mother she'd found a book about me.

Dwarf Longnose was a children's book about Jacob, the shoemaker's son. An evil fairy had used an enchanted herb to change Jacob into a dwarf with a hunched back and a long nose. Jacob's family had thrown him out, and Jacob had become a successful chef in a duke's palace. A goose helped him find the herb to turn him back to normal.

"This is *not* a book about Little Little!" my mother had yelled at Cowboy. "Don't you ever bring a book like this home again!"

"Little Little doesn't have a hunched back"—my father.

"Or a long nose!" my mother said. "Cowboy, you are just as mean as you can be! Look at the pictures in this book! Is that what you think your sister looks like?"

My father had the book removed from the La Belle library, and poor Cowboy never dared check out another library book.

In one of her suicide attempts, when she swallowed down a combination of Dristan and Midol, then ran into the living room to say good-bye to our parents, she sobbed out all the injustices she'd suffered through as my sister. Bringing home that book and catching hell for it was at the top of her list.

We'd laughed about it later; and when my mother began giving parties last summer for the TADpoles, always checking out ahead of time who was p.f. and who wasn't, we'd giggled to each other that the only way Dwarf Longnose would get invited would be if he had royal blood or wanted to be a doctor or a lawyer or the chef who had the in with the goose.

I thought about all that and decided not to give Cowboy a hard time over the remark, so I sat up in bed in time to see her run the left leg of her panty hose because she hadn't cut her big toenail.

"*¢&%$#@!" Cowboy said.

"I told you to cut your toenails. They're so long they're curling over."

"If they were curling over, I wouldn't have run my stocking, Little Little. . . . *Tanoshii tanjobi.*"

"Stick to English."

"There's a whole tableful of gifts for you downstairs, and Little Lion sent white roses."

Cowboy ripped off the panty hose and went across to her bureau drawer to rummage through it for another pair. The long ash at the end of her cigarette dropped into the sock pile she'd shoved aside. The white bra she had on, with the little red bow at the V, had nothing filling it. My mother made her wear the bra when she wore a dress. That was one of my mother's convictions: a bra goes with a dress, just as gloves went with church and something red was worn on Christmas.

"Well, what's he like?" Cowboy said.

"You'd like him," I said. "He doesn't have a long nose, he has a long tooth. And he reads really depressing stuff. On the way to The Palace last night he told me about this short story called 'The Dwarf' by Ray Bradbury." I got out of bed and looked in my closet for something to wear. "This dwarf keeps going to this house of mirrors in this carnival so he can see himself reflected with a tall body. One day they trick him and change the mirror to one that makes everything look really tiny, and he's so shocked he tries to kill himself."

"Neat!" Cowboy said.

"He uses a pistol, though, not Dristan or Midol."

"Well, most men don't have Midol around," Cowboy said. She gave me a wink.

The ash at the end of her Camel was almost an inch long. There were cigarette ashes everywhere in our room, inside drawers, on the rug, on the floor, on the tables, everywhere Cowboy'd passed. Our nearsighted mother never seemed to see them, and Mrs. Hootman never mentioned them because she thought *I* was the smoker, being the older.

She'd clean them away cheerfully, then catch me up in

145

her arms and hug me, while she whispered into my ear, "You *know* you can get away with murder, don't you, Little Missy? But you have to be careful of those teeny-tiny lungs of yours, you know."

This time while Cowboy pushed her leg through the panty hose she curled her big toe under.

"I'm not going to wear white," I said, picking out a pink dress. "I'm not going to look like something off the top of a wedding cake when I get with Little Lion."

"Which one do you like best?" Cowboy said.

"That's a dumb question," I said. "I just went to a movie with him."

"Half a movie," said Cowboy.

"He probably doesn't ever want to see me again. If you were him and you were going to a movie with me and my father rushed down and carried me off caveman style and told him there was a taxi stand across the street, would you ever want to see me again?"

"I'd rise to the challenge," said Cowboy. "I'd think of something dramatic to do. I'd wait until your birthday was under way and then I'd come dancing in under my shell, with my music playing 'La Cu-ca-ra-cha' "—she did a little dance step in her panty hose—" 'la cu-ca-ra-cha,' and crash your party in a burst of glory. Would that impress you?"

"ROACH! ROACH! ROACH!" I chanted the way the crowds had at the game, and Cowboy and I chased each other around the room, laughing.

"Well, it could happen," Cowboy said. Off the floor of

146

her closet, she fished a blue skirt that was always balled up there next to her hockey skates. She began brushing off the dustballs on it. "It's your birthday. Anything can happen."

"Cowboy?" I said. "Do you really like Little Lion?"

She was saved from answering by my mother's voice calling out, "Where's my birthday girl?" as she came up the stairs. Cowboy made a dive for the ashtray, emptying it into one of her Nike sneakers, whirling around, and raising the window. I grabbed the Johnson Wax Glade powder air freshener and aimed it at the ceiling where the smoke collected.

My mother sang out, "Hap-py Birth-day to you, Hap-py Birth-day to you—"

"Don't let her in here!" Cowboy said.

"How'm I going to keep her out?"

Cowboy gave me a shove. "Pretend you're on your way to the bathroom!"

My mother opened the door and said, "Whew! Whew! Girls! Someone's got on too much perfume."

Cowboy said, "After God took his paintbrush to the leaves, he took his powder puff to our bedroom."

"Cowboy," said my mother, "I call that sassy."

"I call it good," I said. "Imaginative. Poetic."

Cowboy took a bow. "I wrote it in a day," she said.

Sydney Cinnamon

19

Digger looked up at the dark morning sky and said, "It's gonna rain buckets in about two seconds. Hurry, Roach!"

I was practically leaping to catch up with him, both of us sweating in our good suits from the ride up to Lake Road and back in the muggy heat.

There was a banner strung across the front of the church reading:

WELCOME LITTLE LION!

WELCOME TADS, TADPOLES, AND PODS!

The street was lined with traffic and policemen trying to control it.

"We're probably too late to make it inside," said Digger.

But we got in, during the choir's singing of "Over There Where the Heathens Are Dying."

Digger had to stand up in the back with other standees,

but an usher led me down front and squeezed me in beside some TADs and TADpoles.

"Little Lion's on next," he whispered at me, smiling.

In addition to all the people packing the church, an overflow crowd was contained in the basement, where loudspeakers were set up.

The first thing I saw after I got seated was an enormous white ladder set up beside the pulpit. It was strung with white roses, and under each rung there was a sign, so it looked like this:

100%—I DID!

90%—I WILL!

80%—I CAN!

70%—I THINK I CAN!

60%—I MIGHT!

50%—I THINK I MIGHT!

40%—WHAT IS IT?

30%—I WISH I COULD!

20%—I DON'T KNOW HOW!

10%—I CAN'T!

0%—I WON'T!

While the choir sang, Reverend La Belle sat in a throne chair behind the pulpit. In the front of the pulpit there was a bouquet of white crysanthemums in a brass urn. A white ribbon was pinned to the flowers, and across it in gold was L I T T L E   L I O N.

The dwarf beside me was balancing a ten-gallon hat on his knees.

He turned to me while the choir was singing and whispered, "I'm Gus Gregory," holding out his hand. "Little's better, less is more."

I shook his hand. "Sydney Cinnamon," I said. "What's better?"

"Little's better, less is more. Aren't you a TAD or a TADpole?"

"Not yet," I said.

"That's our slogan," he said.

I was wiggling around in my seat, craning my neck to try and find Little Little in the crowd.

"Little Lion won't come from the back," said Gus Gregory. "He'll come from behind the curtains up front."

Then, as though that was his cue, the choir began "Just As I Am," there was movement behind the purple curtains, and Little Lion stepped out.

"Just as I am, tho' tossed about," the choir continued bravely, drowned out by the applause, *"With many a conflict, many a doubt."*

Gus Gregory was standing on the red cushions of the pew, swinging his sky piece, and others in our aisle stood on their seats, too.

"Fightings and fears within, without," the choir persisted, *"O Lamb of God, I come, I come."*

Little Lion was resplendent in white from top to bottom, complete with a white rosebud boutonniere.

As he walked toward the white ladder, he held up his

hands to try and stop the applause, but there was no way. There were even whistles.

The choir was relentless:

"Just as I am, and waiting not,
To rid my soul of one dark blot."

I stood on my seat in the excitement and finally spotted Little Little, sitting on something that elevated her, between her mother and father. She was wearing pink, a white rose pinned to the collar of her dress. She was in a middle row, clapping and smiling while I did hypnosis on her: *Look my way,* and flopped. She continued looking straight ahead at Little Lion.

Little Lion was climbing the ladder.

The crowd was calming down; the choir was coming through again:

"O Lamb of God, I come! I come!"

When Little Lion reached the top of the ladder, Reverend La Belle stepped forward.

He said, "Little Lion is at the top of the Ladder of Achievement, ready to share his thoughts with you. Having him with us this Sunday morning is a great achievement for us! Little Lion?"

Then there were a few minutes more of applause while Reverend La Belle disappeared through the curtains, and Little Lion stood on 90%—I WILL!, with his hands holding firmly to 100%—I DID!

"The best lesson I ever learned, I learned from an oyster," Little Lion began. "Up here in lake country, I don't know if you know about oysters. Up here in the beautiful Finger Lakes of New York State, I doubt you think very much about oysters . . . unless you're going out somewheres fancy to eat a gourmet dinner, and then maybe you think about oysters. Oysters Rockefeller, with the spinach and the celery and the Parmesan cheese, fancied-up oysters that'll give you a taste thrill for some five, six, seven dollars or *more* now in these inflated times!

"Oysters. Up here in the beautiful Finger Lakes of New York State you don't think about oysters, do you? Unless you're hungry and your taste buds are telling you ooooooh I'd like an oyster, like one on the half shell, like one with a little horseradish sauce, like one with a wedge of lemon to squeeze over it, like an oyster on the half shell, iced, sitting in a bed of crisp, cool lettuce. An oyster.

"Well now, you didn't come here this morning for this, to hear about oysters, up here in the beautiful Finger Lakes of New York State, say what the heck is that dwarf doing talking about an oyster, Sunday morning, church . . . oyster? Oyster?"

Little Lion looked out at us, all around the room, so silent you could hear a pin drop. He ran his hand over his red curly hair.

Then he shouted, "Yes, an oyster!"

And the heavens above collaborated with him: Lightning flashed at the long, thin windows of the church.

"An oyster is an extraordinary creature, in case you don't

152

know about oysters up here in lake country. Up here in lake country you've got a lot of problems and I know it. I know you have! You step outside your door every morning to face them: Your kids are leaving this town because there's no industry to employ them, nothing to keep them here. Your kids are going to school and they're finding pot, marijuana, right there in the recess yard along with the slides and swings, grass that isn't the kind you walk on, but the kind that clouds the mind! You have problems up here in the beautiful Finger Lakes. I know you have!"

There was more lightning.

Little Lion looked up as though the heavens were exclaiming with him and nodded.

"You got in-law problems, and outlaw problems, and you can't communicate with your wife, and your husband drinks, and your mother is old now and feeble, and your best friend and you have lost touch, and your parents criticize you all the time without ever asking to hear your side. They don't want to hear it, sometimes it seems they don't give a plugged nickel for your side, just everyone's but yours. You get so darned discouraged with everything that's going on, you could die! I know it. Lord, *I* know it."

Little Lion stepped down to 80%—I CAN!

"What's the sense of it all, anyway?"

He stepped down to 70%—I THINK I CAN!

He said, "What's the point of it all? You tell me."

It began to rain, a hard windy rain that beat against the church windows. He went down to the next rung and said,

153

"Faith? Faith in what? You tell me."

He went down to 50%—I THINK I MIGHT! "Love? Speak up, I didn't quite catch the word. Love? Did you say love? What's love? Hah? You tell me."

Another rung down. Beside me, Gus Gregory was clutching his hat so tightly his knuckles had turned red.

"It's all turned against me, see. How do you cope when it all goes against you? How? You tell me."

On 30%—I WISH I COULD!, Little Lion paused, removed a white handkerchief from his pocket, put it to his face, held it there, put it back. Then he sobbed out, "Don't console me! I'm tired of it. Don't pacify me! I've had it! Don't lead me on and on and on because where am I going? I don't want to keep going until I know where I'm going. . . . You tell me."

Little Lion moved down to the next rung. "O Lord, where'd you go? Were you ever here or was that all just so much . . . talk," the last word very softly. "Was it all just talk? Were you ever interested in me? Me, Lord. Me! Are you around for me? You tell me."

Little Lion stepped to 10% and stood there silently.

Then he said, "The most extraordinary thing about the oyster is this. He doesn't have to go out and find his problems. He's got them built in! Irritations! Irritations! They're as much a part of him as my heart or my liver or my lungs are a part of me. How does he stand living with those irritations built right into his shell?"

Little Lion stepped down to 0%—I WON'T! He shook his

head and said in a humming whine that began a great sob, "You tell me!"

Then he stepped away from the ladder.

He walked slowly to the front of the podium.

"He tries to get rid of the irritations. Oh, God, how he tries! He tries to get rid of them and he tries to get rid of them and oh, God, they don't go away! They won't go away. They are there to stay. They are as much a part of him as my heart or my liver or my lungs!

"He says go away, get out, go, leave me, please, go! But they are there to stay!

"Now listen to what he does. Listen to what this oyster does. This extraordinary creature doesn't ask what's the point of it all! He doesn't say anything about faith in *what*—he's got enough faith to fill an ocean! He doesn't say, What's love? He doesn't ask how to cope, or where he's going, or how he's going to get there, and he doesn't question the Lord!

"I'll tell you what he does, and how he knew to do it, you tell me.

"I'll tell you what he does!

"When he cannot get rid of his irritations he settles down to make them into one of the most beautiful things in this world. He uses the irritations to do the loveliest thing that an oyster ever has a chance to do!

"If there are irritations in your life, take an example from the oyster, my friends, and make a pearl.

"Make a pearl. . . ." He stared out at us. "Have you got

the love? Have you got the faith? . . . You . . . tell . . . me."
Then the choir began singing:

> *"Throw out the lifeline across the dark wave,*
> *There is a brother whom someone should save. . . ."*

"Will you walk up here to me, friends?" Little Lion began. "Walk up here for a blessing. Who will walk up here now for Christ?"

> *"Throw out the lifeline, throw out the lifeline,*
> *Someone is drifting away,*
> *Throw out the lifeline, throw out the lifeline,*
> *Someone is sinking to-day.*

Dwarfs and normals began filing up the aisles as the choir continued and Little Lion shouted above it, "You know who I mean. There's someone special here who needs this blessing, and you know who you are. I am talking to you directly now and you know it's you I mean. And you know you're special, and you know I've reached you, and why aren't you walking down here to me? I'm going to keep after you until you do. I'm going to wait for you."

Digger and Laura Gwen went past me with the babies, and Gus Gregory left his hat on his seat and squeezed past my legs.

I looked over my shoulder to see Little Little settled back in her seat, watching.

Little Lion's voice rose even higher. "You know who you are! Can't I reach you? Aren't you coming? Don't you care?"

156

There was no special expression on Little Little's face.

"You can shout, 'I'll walk with you, Little Lion,' " Little Lion barked. "I wish you would. I wish you'd shout it out and come down here to walk with me!"

At first some people mumbled it, and then gathered courage and called it out, "I'll walk with you, Little Lion."

Little Lion had his handkerchief back out and was almost crying now, while he shouted, "What will it take to move you? O Lord, what do you want me to do? I'm trying everything I know! I'm breaking my heart here trying to get you to walk with me. Don't you want to? Won't you tell me that you want to and come forward? Please? Don't you want to? Can't you tell me that you want to?"

I kept looking over my shoulder to be sure Little Little hadn't gotten down to go up the aisle.

Practically everyone in the church had, and they were lined up at the front, the TADs and TADpoles invited up to the stage to stand behind Little Lion.

"Who else?" Little Lion yelled out, his voice hoarse. "You know who you are! Oh, why won't you do it? Don't you want to? Won't you tell me that you do?"

There was a sudden bolt of thunder, and then a female voice shrieked, "I do, Little Lion!"

I turned to see her dancing up the aisle, as I had seen her dance across my television screen so many times: Dora, minus her lettuce leaf.

Even Little Lion looked surprised.

Little Little La Belle

20

"Little Little," said Little Lion, "I want you to meet Eloise Ficklin, also known as Dora, The Dancing Lettuce Leaf."

"Oh, happy happy days," my mother sang. *"When I lie down I'll have a coat of golden mayonnaise."*

"We've met," I said.

"We have? Where?"

"In Pennsylvania at a TADpole party. You were in the motel pool at the deep end and you told me you could stand at that end, that you weren't one of us."

"Well now, Little Little, you have the *best* memory!" Eloise Ficklin exclaimed. "I don't remember meeting you at all."

We were gathered in Grandfather La Belle's study, at the back of the church, waiting for the crowds to thin out and the street in front to clear of traffic.

Grandfather La Belle had gone around back to the parking lot to bring my father's car to the side door. Then we were all going to head for our house, for a light lunch before the banquet later that afternoon.

Eloise Ficklin was sticking to Little Lion like glue, dressed all in white the same as he was, and plucking his boutonniere from his lapel for a souvenir.

"I don't know what I'm going to do about this rain," she cooed down at him. "This rain is going to just ruin my hair."

"I'll tell you what," said Little Lion. "I was going to leave my car behind the church so the Faithful wouldn't get hurt mobbing it as they do. But they're nearly all gone, and I could run you to where you're going, and then drive up to the La Belles'."

"Oh, I wouldn't *hear* of that, Little Lion!"

"We can drop you on our way," said my father.

"Now, I wouldn't hear of *that,* sir," Little Lion said to my father. "I will just back out my new little white Mercedes convertible quick as a wink and do the honors. It'll be no trouble at all."

Eloise Ficklin said, "Let me tell my manager that he can go on without me. Oh, it'll be a relief to him, we spend so much time together! Are you *sure* it won't be an imposition, Little Lion?"

"I'll be delighted to do it," said Little Lion, and my mother shot me one of her looks.

Little Lion grabbed my hand as Eloise Ficklin darted out of the study.

"Hallelujah, honey, it's good to be with you at last!" He picked up our joined hands and kissed my knuckles. "I kept waiting for you to walk with me. You know that was what I was waiting for all along."

"Little Little won't walk with anyone," said my mother. "She's too independent."

"Well, life turns out strange sometimes. I was anticipating climaxing my service with my Little Little walking with me, and I got Dora instead."

"She's very tall for a diminutive," said my mother. "She's a good head taller than you are, Little Lion."

"I will lift up mine eyes," Little Lion answered.

"Little Lion," said my father, "you might tell Little Little that the carriage awaits. Granddaddy's sitting out there in it, in the rain. I'd tell Little Little myself, only she seems not to hear anything I have to say this morning."

"Now, we are not going to wash the family linen out in public, Larry," said my mother. "Somebody better go find Cowboy and Mock."

"I'll go find them," my father said. "We'll see you at the house, young man."

"I would ask you to ride along with us, Little Little," Little Lion said to me, "but there's only room for two."

"And Dora is a big girl besides," said my mother. "It'd take several coats of mayonnaise to cover her."

Little Lion laughed and squeezed my hand. "I trust she's invited to the banquet?"

"She's not on the list," said my mother.

160

"We can make room," I said.

"Honey, I would love nothing more than to include her but we're not having chicken à la king or anything like that. We're having slices of beef Wellington, and I've already made room for Norman Powers' mother who wasn't expected, plus that dear little tyke from Mineola, New York, who showed up unexpectedly."

"She can have my slice of beef Wellington," I said.

"When it's your favorite thing in the whole world, honey? Why, we planned it especially for your birthday," said my mother, shooting me another one of her looks.

"We'll manage," I said.

"Nothing is impossible to a willing heart," Little Lion said.

My mother said, "All lay load on the willing horse."

"I like your sense of humor, Mrs. La Belle," said Little Lion.

On the way home in our car, my mother said, "That little snip. If she's a diminutive, I'm a Siamese twin."

I sat in back, on my Kiddyride, between Mock and Cowboy.

Cowboy whispered at me, "That was him next to Gus Gregory, wasn't it?"

I nodded.

"He kept watching you over his shoulder," she said.

I said, "I know it."

My mother was continuing her diatribe. "Little Little, now is the time to fight fire with fire. Telling him to ask her to the banquet was a major mistake, but—"

"Whose idea was that?" my father asked.

"It was his idea," said my mother, "but Little Little went right along with it, which was a major mistake."

"Maybe Little Little isn't all that taken with him in the ninth place," said my father. "I'm not all that taken with him."

"You wouldn't be all that taken with Prince Charming if he rode right up Lake Road on a white horse with a wedding ring in a box in his back pocket," my mother said. "You'd keep her in a hothouse the same as Grandfather La Belle keeps his prize roses in one, if you had your way."

"If we were speaking, I would," said my father.

"Well, we aren't," I said.

Mock Hiroyuki giggled and my mother told him, "There is nothing funny in this situation, in case anyone should ride up on a bicycle and ask you. That little snip is pushing her way into Little Little's birthday celebration."

Mock clapped his hands across his mouth and sank down beside me on the backseat.

"I'm not all that taken with him, either," Cowboy said.

"Aren't you?" I said.

"Not all that taken with him."

"Well, I doubt very much that Cowboy is anyone to judge who is and who isn't a catch," said my mother.

"Are you?" my father asked her.

"Well, I caught you, didn't I? In my opinion, Little Little," said my mother, turning around from the front seat to see me better, "you should go home and put on that pretty little light-blue dress Mrs. Hootman made for you last summer, and come out fighting, beginning at lunch. I don't know why in the world you didn't walk with him this morning, when it was obvious to everyone in that church he was waiting for someone special, calling out to her that way. Why, that was *painful!*"

"I'm not religious," I said.

"The whole thing was painful!" Cowboy said.

My father said, "A-men."

My mother turned back in the front seat and stared at the road, sighing and shaking her head. She said to my father, "Would you rather have her with The Roach, Larry?"

"I'd rather not have her with either of them."

"Oh, don't we know that! You'd rather have her to yourself."

"The way I see it," said my father, "there's just no damn hurry, Ava. She's got time. She's only eighteen."

"I remember when that little Blessing girl from Cleveland took her time deciding whether or not to marry that little Tompkins boy who was studying to be a doctor. Before she knew it he turned around and married what's-her-name who won the TADpole chess tournament every year."

"Oh, don't start in on that little Blessing girl again," said my father.

"She's still living at home and she's in her twenties now," my mother said. "All we're talking about here is a full happy life, with a family, all that anyone's entitled to."

"That's all *you're* talking about here," said my father. "We aren't talking about it."

"Mock?" Cowboy said. "Do Japanese families bicker all the time?"

"Bery often bicka," said Mock.

"Mock," my mother said, "we are *not* bickering. We just want what's best for Little Little."

"We want her to do the loveliest thing that an oyster ever has a chance to do," Cowboy said.

"They want me to make a pearl, Mock," I said.

"I'm glad everyone in the backseat thinks that's hilarious," said my mother.

When we got inside the house, the white wicker giraffe was waiting for me next to my walnut *sgabello* in the hall.

"*What* is this?" My mother's face broke into a delighted smile. "It has a card around its neck. Honey, I'll read it for you. . . . It says, 'I long for you.' The long neck! I long for you! Now, darling, that is what I call original! Isn't that original?"

I stood up on the *sgabello* and read the card myself. There were only those four words across it.

"Is that from Little Lion?" said my father.

"Who else?" my mother said. "Now, there's someone after my own heart. Original, amusing, poignant, too, there's something very poignant about it—that dear little

164

darling, and here this was waiting for you all the while he was standing there begging you practically on bended knee to come down the aisle and walk with him."

"Mrs. La Belle?" Mrs. Hootman appeared in the doorway.

"Yes, Mrs. Hootman, just a minute. Little Little?" my mother said. "This is a very touching gift if you ask me, which I realize no one did."

"No one ever has to," my father said.

"And even you, Larry, have to admit this is a dear little birthday remembrance. You yourself never matched this in all the time you were courting me, and you weren't unoriginal."

"Thank you," said my father.

"So, honey, you put on that little sky-blue dress Mrs. Hootman made for you (of all her dresses, Mrs. Hootman, that's my favorite) and you get yourself ready for Little Lion. He went to all this trouble to have this waiting for you."

"Mrs. La Belle?" Mrs. Hootman tried again.

"Yes, Mrs. Hootman?"

"That giraffe isn't from Little Lion."

It was five-thirty when they entered the pantry. The banquet was running late. The waiters were just clearing away the dinner plates. I was resting, out of sight so I'd be a surprise. I was stretched out on top of a sack of Magic Mashed Potato Flakes, in the storeroom just behind the pantry.

"Dora"—I heard Little Lion's voice—"the Lord sent you to me."

"Eloise," she corrected him.

"Eloise, the Lord sent you to me."

"I hate that Little Little La Belle! I hated her when I first met her and I still hate her!"

"This is not a time to talk of hatred, hon. Hallelujah!"

"I hate these TADpole affairs, too. You don't know how many I've been dragged to by my parents, and PODs is a good name for my parents, because they *are* pods! If

I'd been one inch *taller* than normal, they'd have gone through the Yellow Pages looking for an organization of giants!"

"Walk with me, I was begging, and you came down that aisle toward me with the face of a Botticelli angel, with your golden hair."

"Don't touch it, please, because I can't get a wash and set tomorrow morning, and I have a real early appointment. . . . I couldn't believe it when I went to that church to hear you, and there *they* all were—the Munchkins!"

"I have a great many dwarfs among the Faithful, Dora, being a dwarf myself."

"Eloise," she corrected him again. "Well, *I'm* four foot one!"

"Every inch a beauty!"

"That little shrimp doesn't think her own pee smells."

"Dora, Eloise—never mind Little Little right now."

"Don't tell me *she's* your girl friend? A dynamite little guy like you?"

"Eloise, a man of God needs many inspirations. Where do you go from here?"

"You've got big hands for such a little fellow, don't you? I'm making supermarket appearances in the Tri-State Area for my client."

"These hands do the Lord's work."

"Is that what you call it?" She chuckled.

"Where are you going next?"

"I'm due at the Super-Duper Market on Salina Street in

Syracuse, nine-thirty tomorrow morning. Oh, darlin', be real careful of my hair, hmmm?"

"Will you be at the Inn tonight?"

"Do you want me to be at the Inn tonight, Little Love?"

"Hallelujah, babe!"

"Well, hallelujah yourself, Preacher."

They stopped talking for a while and I didn't have to see them to know what they were up to. I sat up on the sack of Magic Mashed Potato Flakes, moving as quietly as I could, easing my stocking feet down until they touched the floor.

"I've seen you on television," she said.

"I've seen you, too."

"I saw you on *The Powerful Hour.*"

"I used to turn on the set just to wait for you to come on. Sometimes you did"—*smack, smack*—"and sometimes you didn't."

"You pulling my leg?"

"Not yet."

"I really mean it about my hair, hon. It's been so darn humid here all day, too."

There was a pause in the conversation while I inched my way past the potato sack toward the door.

Then she said, "I hate her hair. Looks like a monkey styles it."

"We don't have to talk about her," Little Lion said.

"The same monkey that does her hair makes her clothes, if you ask me."

"Honey? Babe? Give yourself to the moment and don't be worrying your angel's head about another female."

"They're going to be serving that little insect her birthday cake any minute, Little Love."

"What time *is* it?"

"How'm I going to not worry my head about another female if you're going to worry yours about what time they present that ugly cake to that little gnat all dressed in baby blue?"

"Well, I am a guest of the family, my angel."

"I say let's us vamoose and the hell with her and her cake."

"Well, now—"

"You could get our coats and I could just slip out the back and be waiting for you in your car."

"Oh, babe, the devil tempts the mighty with the answer to his prayers, and how does the mighty resist? You tell me."

Just as I peered around the doorway, I saw Reverend La Belle charging through the swinging doors of the kitchen. I ducked back inside the storeroom.

"Little Lion! Here you are!"

"Hello, Reverend! You know Dora . . . Eloise. It's time to carry the cake in, and Eloise here has promised to help me do the honors."

"The honors are overdue, Little Lion! . . . How do you do, miss."

"Well, we'll do the overdue honors then, Reverend,"

said Dora. "I was just saying to Little Lion how pretty that little granddaughter of yours is!"

"Cake's heavy!" Reverend La Belle barked.

"All lay load on the willing horse," said Little Lion.

"And I'd like a word with you first, Little Lion," said the Reverend. "Alone."

"I'll just wait in the kitchen," said Dora, "like a good little lettuce leaf." She chuckled.

"Little Lion," Reverend La Belle said after the sound of the kitchen door swinging shut, "my granddaughter takes second place to no one!"

"Amen, sir."

"A little girl like that, living protected as she has, isn't going to get up and waltz down the aisle to walk with any man, eloquent as his plea might be. If you don't know that, you don't know dogs bark!"

"I know that now, sir."

"Performers get up and perform, but shy little girls who aren't selling mayonnaise for a living are reluctant to step forward. Now you have to make up your mind whether what you want is a snappy saleswoman a head taller than you are or a shy young miss your same size. . . . Seems to me all through the banquet you were veering toward the former."

"Reverend, my heart follows after the meek—"

Reverend La Belle cut him off with "Don't give me a lot of crap, Little Lion. If you want to become affianced to my granddaughter, you better act that way before I bust ass!"

From inside the ballroom the band began to play "Happy Birthday."

I put on my shoes, got my shell out, and dragged it through the swinging doors to the kitchen, after the singing began.

Waiters stepped around me, stacking the dinner dishes near the dishwasher, while I waited and watched through a crack in the door leading into the ballroom.

Dora and Little Lion were carrying a three-tiered cake across the ballroom floor to the front table. The candles were flickering as they went slowly along, the silver platter between them, headed toward Little Little, who was seated at the end of the table.

While everyone sang chorus after chorus, Little Little crawled down from her chair and walked across to meet them.

There was applause, then cheers and whistles.

Little Little looked out at everyone all smiles, her long yellow hair hanging down to brush the light blue dress, her light green eyes sparkling. The band began to play "For She's a Jolly Good Fellow" as the cake came toward her.

Then Dora, The Dancing Lettuce Leaf, appeared to begin to dance, but stumbled instead, tipping the tray sufficiently to deliver the gooey white coconut cake directly to Little Little, all down the front of her.

What was left landed at her feet, as the tray spun around

the floor like a top, before it flopped flat.

There was a loud, communal Ohhhhhhhhhhhhhhh.

The dwarf who had sat beside me in church jumped down to stamp out a few burning candles with his feet.

Little Little began to run. She ran down the length of the ballroom floor, heading straight toward the kitchen.

She stumbled in past me, tripped over my roach shell, and landed on the linoleum, where she sat with pieces of cake, and sticky frosting, and a single candle stuck to her.

"Has anyone got a match?" I said, and a waiter handed me an oven match.

I struck it, reached down and removed the candle from the front of Little Little, wiped the wick clean with my fingers, and lit it.

"Make a wish," I said.

Little Little La Belle

". . . and that was the Ramones singing 'Baby, I Love You.' This is WLAB in beautiful La Belle, and we'll be with you for another two hours spinning your favorite tunes. The time is seven-ten, and the temperature's rising to the thirties on this first day of November."

Cowboy is smoking before breakfast again. I hear the scratch of a match and catch my first whiff of tobacco as I roll over on top of a book I'd been reading before I fell asleep.

"Are your spirits laggin'? Come to The Pink Dragon and watch the steel ball fall into the lucky hole that'll win you a vacation trip for two to beautiful Hawaii, or a brand-new Toyota! These are just a few of the rewards awaiting you at La Belle's newest fun spot on Genesee Street, where there are sixty-one pin tables and over a hundred prizes! Yes, pachinko is here in La Belle, and The Pink Dragon himself will be on hand afternoons to welcome you! They say dragons are lucky. . . ."

"Turn it down, Cowboy!"

"Does he like being The Pink Dragon better or Roy Roachers?"

"I don't know," I say, "I've never asked him."

I sit up in bed and rub the sleep from my eyes. I toss *The Tin Drum* on the night table, remembering where I'd left off the night before. Oskar, the dwarf hero, went to see a Christmas play, *Tom Thumb*. Only you never saw Tom Thumb onstage. You just heard his voice and saw people chasing after him. He sits inside a horse's ear, crawls in a mousehole and a snail shell. He gets in a cow's stomach and a wolf's stomach.

At the end of the play, when Tom Thumb names all the places he's been and says, "Now I'm coming home to you," Oskar's mother hides her nose in her handkerchief, and then can't stop hugging him all through the holidays.

Sounds like my mother when she's minty.

Cowboy is pulling on her jeans and cussing about basketball practice keeping her from seeing The Pink Dragon in action.

"Don't you see enough of him?" I ask her.

"You don't seem to," she says.

I am remembering that it is Friday, the day Miss Grossman hands back our writing assignments.

I am betting that no matter what Calpurnia Dove has written, my true story of a dwarf named Lia Graf will be the one Miss Grossman reads in class.

Weeks of research have gone into it. It has everything: bathos, pathos, even Hitler.

Lia Graf, whose real name was Schwartz, was a world-famous twenty-seven-inch dwarf who'd appeared with Ringling Bros. and Barnum & Bailey Circus. When she was twenty years old she'd even sat on the lap of the richest man in America, J. P. Morgan, while he was testifying before the Senate Banking Committee. Wearing a blue satin dress and a bright-red straw hat, she perched there as photographers snapped their picture. Someone had put her up to it, in an attempt to embarrass Morgan, but he rose to the occasion and told her he had a grandson bigger than she was.

She came to a sad end in a Nazi concentration camp, doomed not only because she was a Jew but also because she was a dwarf. The Nazis were embarked on a program to destroy all people who were physically abnormal.

It was Sydney Cinnamon who told me about her and helped me do the research in the La Belle library.

It was Sydney Cinnamon who got me to check out *The Tin Drum*, too.

Today I dress carefully in a blue wool number Mrs. Hootman made for me, as I plan to be the center of attention at approximately two o'clock in the afternoon.

At breakfast my father complains about having to go to a Lions' Club luncheon, which means trying to park on Genesee Street, impossible because of all the $%#¢& congestion caused by The Pink Dragon.

"Wait until the geisha girls get here!" says my mother, who is thumbing through the latest edition of *The TADpole Tattler.*

"Cowboy, don't wear your hat at the breakfast table!" my father snaps.

"Don't wear it at the lunch table or the dinner table, either," says my mother. "Someday you're going to wake up and that hat's going to be missing."

Then my mother's face lights up and she says, "Little Little, listen to this! You remember that sweet little tyke from Mineola who dropped into your birthday party unexpectedly and I was worried that we didn't have enough beef Wellington?"

"Naomi Katz," I said. "What about her?"

"She and Roderick Wentworth are hosting a joint New Year's Eve party to be held down in Miami, Florida. Oh, how I would love to go to Florida!"

"Too bad you're not a TADpole," Cowboy says.

"The PODs are invited, too," says my mother, "and Roderick Wentworth is p.f. and planning to be a CPA."

"Wow!" Cowboy says. "A p.f. CPA!"

"I'm not directing this conversation to *you*, Cowboy."

"Don't direct it to me, either," I say. "Roderick Wentworth has chronic halitosis."

"Something that can be *corrected*," says my mother.

"Did you tell Mrs. Hootman we're having company for dinner?" I ask her.

"I told her," says my mother.

My father looks up and asks, "Who?"

"Oh, guess," says my mother. "Just guess."

"He's more like a permanent fixture around here," says

my father. "I see him around here as often as I see the oven in the kitchen and the walnut *sgabello* in the hall!"

"And Mock," I say. "You see him as often as you see Mock Hiroyuki."

"That's not by choice, either," he mumbles into his fried eggs.

"Well, it's not my choice to spend all winter locked into snow country," my mother says. "I would *love* a Florida vacation, and here we have the golden opportunity right in front of us. You know the Wentworths, Larry. He's in mobile homes."

"Little Little says his breath smells."

"I'm talking about his father! His father's in mobile homes!"

On and on.

Cowboy is riding to school on the back of Mock's new moped. My mother is bumming a ride to her Creative Crafts Coffee Klatch with me. Her car is in Ace Garage. She backed it into an oak tree at the end of our driveway, and saved the tiny red glass pieces of the smashed taillight, telling me she'd use them in a collage she is planning to make. A truly imaginative person, she says, can always find the beauty.

As I drive her down Lake Road, she says in another month we won't even be able to see the lake over the snowdrifts, and that there's a hotel in Miami that runs an elevator outside the building, with an angel for an elevator operator, "wings and all."

"I don't want to leave school," I say; "my English class is just getting interesting."

"I wonder if that's the real reason you don't want to leave, Little Little."

"Well, it's one of them."

"And the other?"

"There are a lot of others. I like snow, besides."

"Snow? You like snow? All I do is worry about you falling in some snowdrift and you sit up there on your little seat and tell me you *like* it?"

We ride along in silence for a while until she musters up the courage to come to the real point.

"Little Lion was a mistake," she says, "but you correct a mistake, you don't compound it with another one."

"Meaning what?"

"Meaning don't get all caught up with this Cinnamon character."

"Boy," I say. "He's not a character."

"Well, he's running around as a dragon one minute and appearing as a roach cowboy on the television the next, you don't think of him as a boy, you think of him as a character."

"I think of him as a boy."

"He's been to dinner three Friday nights in a row, honey."

"Mock has, too."

"Oh, *Mock* . . . Mock's just a friend. Cowboy's young, and Mock's young, not at a point where they're supposed to be planning what they'd like to do with their lives. Honey, all

I'm saying to you is that I'd give my eyes to see you walk down the aisle on the arm of some nice, serious young man who wants to make something out of himself."

"How could you see me do that without your eyes?" I say.

"I might as well talk to that telephone pole up ahead," she says. "But I know one thing I would do, if I were you, Little Little."

"What's that?"

"Well, if you're going to be seeing him for whatever little interlude it takes you to get tired of him, you ought to speak to him about his tooth. Now, *that's* something that can be corrected. That tooth of his sticks out too far."

"Can't you ever get past that thing you have about physical appearances?" I said. "If Mozart had a pimple on his nose, you wouldn't even be able to hear his music. You'd just be sitting there wishing you could squeeze the pimple!"

"I would never squeeze anyone else's pimple, Little Little!"

"You know what I mean," I tell her, yelling. "If Shakespeare had a hair coming out of his nose, you wouldn't hear a word of one of his plays—you'd be wondering why he didn't take a tweezer to it!"

"Slow down and stop shouting!"

"If Pablo Picasso had a wart on his finger, he wouldn't be the world-famous painter in your eyes, he'd be that fellow with the wart on his finger who paints! You are all caught up in and bogged down in p.f.! Sydney Cinnamon has one of the best minds of anyone who's ever sat down at our dinner table and all you see is the tooth that sticks out!"

"That's not all I see," my mother says.

"The hump, the tooth that sticks out, the twisted leg—you never see anyone's real worth!"

"But he can go right down to Dr. Rosten and get that tooth fixed in an afternoon, honey, that's all I'm saying. That tooth is something he can correct."

"Why *should he*?"

"Stop getting yourself into such a snit right after breakfast," my mother says. "It's not good for the digestion, and don't go past my stop."

"I hope there's nobody in your Creative Crafts Coffee Klatch with a mole on her nose or anything disgusting like that," I say.

"There isn't," she says. "And thank you for the ride. Next time I'll think a long time before I decide to share a little feeling with you I might have about improving someone's appearance."

"Promises. Promises," I tell her, stopping the car. *"Sayonara."*

"Don't go to the pachinko parlor after school, either," she says, getting out. "It's bad enough that The Pink Dragon is at our table every Friday night. Oh, I'm used to him and that isn't a complaint—he's welcome—but a pachinko parlor is no place for a little girl."

She gives me a smile before she shuts the car door. "Oh, honey, I know you're a big girl now. But you're our Little

Little and we love you so much!"

I cross my eyes and blow her a kiss.

"Your eyes could snap and stay that way forever," she tells me. "Then what would you do?"

"Then what would *you* do?"

The morning drags unbearably, and I cannot concentrate on Newton's three laws of motion in science or Gibbon's version of the fall of Rome in history. Even the special assembly, "Marijuana Can Wreck Your Mind," makes me squirm impatiently in my seat, although the school has come up with an ex-con who murdered two men as the lecturer.

On my way out of the auditorium I pass Calpurnia Dove and notice that she is wearing a new pink sweater with a matching skirt and the same color knee-high socks.

At lunch, Sydney Cinnamon has saved me a seat in the back of the cafeteria. He is excited about a book he's reading called *Freddy's Story.*

"Listen to this," he says, wiping away crumbs of tuna fish sandwich from his mouth. "This is when Winesap, the historian, has just finished a lecture on all the Bigfoot creatures that have been sighted all over America. He's being approached by another historian named Agaard, and he says—"

"Sydney," I sigh, "I'd rather read the book myself."

"Just listen to this," he insists the way he always insists. "Agaard comes up to Winesap and he says, 'I have a son home who is a monster.' " Sydney grins over at me. "Isn't that a neat beginning?"

"Neat," I agree.

"Then Agaard invites Winesap home to meet his son, who's eight foot tall!"

"I'll borrow it when you're finished," I say.

Then he starts to tell me about more new things he's bought for his apartment, behind the pachinko parlor. Whenever I go there, he shows me something new he's bought. Once he surprised me with a miniature water bed he'd had custom-made. We stretched out on it and listened to tapes of The Bee Gees, Earth, Wind and Fire, and Haydn's *Surprise* symphony, drinking white wine from new crystal goblets, while he told me Haydn's wife was so mean she used his manuscripts as curlpapers.

He is always enthusiastic about something, but today I am not a good listener.

I am saved from pretending that I am by a quartet of freshmen who surround Sydney Cinnamon to ask for autographs.

"Roy or The Dragon?" he asks them.

"Both!" they chorus in unison.

I finish the date-and-nut sandwich Mrs. Hootman has made me for lunch and count the minutes to English class: one hundred and three.

Finally we are filing into Miss Grossman's room, where she has written across the blackboard in yellow chalk:

True ease in writing comes from art, not chance,
As those move easier who have learn'd to dance.
*   —Alexander Pope*

After all of us are in our seats, Miss Grossman begins handing back everyone's story but the one she'll read.

My mind is still reeling with the sight of my own before me on my desk, marked A+, when Miss Grossman speaks.

"And now," she says, "I want you all to be still and listen to this."

Sickly, I sneak a glance across at Calpurnia Dove, who just as sickly meets my eye, her story clutched in her fingers.

Miss Grossman begins:

" 'Sydney,' Mr. Palmer said, 'you are on your way to becoming the most famous dwarf in the country, no small thanks to me. And now I have a favor to ask you.'

"Those words, spoken on an ordinary August day, in the offices of Palmer Pest Control, were the beginning of my new life. . . ."

While she continues to read, after I have recovered from the punch of shock to my insides, I turn around in my seat and stare at Sydney Cinnamon.

He smiles at me, his light-blue eyes very bright, and gives a helpless shrug to his shoulders.

I decide that my mother is right.

That tooth of his sticks out too far.

183

About the Author

M. E. Kerr was born in Auburn, New York, attended the University of Missouri, and now lives in East Hampton, New York. Ms. Kerr is the author of several novels for young people, her most recent being GENTLEHANDS.